Just a Bit Wrecked

Straight Guys Book 11

Alessandra Hazard

Copyright © 2020 Alessandra Hazard

ISBN: 9798743555840

Table of Contents

Just a Bit Wrecked

PART I

Chapter 1

"Stop staring at them, honey. You're being terribly rude."

Andrew Reyes tore his gaze from the gay couple and looked at his wife. Vivian was frowning at him, disapproval plain on her kind face.

Andrew scowled. "What's rude is that they're practically groping each other in front of us," he hissed. "It's a public place. It's bad enough that we have to sit next to those people for hours, but we don't need to look at that—that indecency."

Vivian chuckled, patting him on his arm. "Indecency? You sound like a Victorian lady from some BBC period drama. It's the twenty-first century, Drew. Let them be."

Andrew glared at his wife, annoyed that she didn't share his annoyance. His gaze returned to the couple they were sharing the first-class cabin with, and he scowled again.

The older man, the one with dark hair and chocolate-brown eyes, was leaned back in his seat, his posture lazy and indulgent. The top two buttons of his blue shirt were unbuttoned, revealing a hint of his muscular chest.

The other guy, a redhead, was practically in his lap, kissing the man's tan neck. Andrew couldn't see his left hand, but he was pretty sure it was under the dark-haired man's shirt. It was absolutely disgusting.

"Stop gawking at them, Andrew," Vivian whispered exasperatedly.

Andrew barely heard her. His gaze followed the redhead's right hand as it trailed down the other man's muscular torso, over his abs, to his belt—

"Gross," Andrew said, snapping his gaze upward.

Brown eyes locked with his. Their owner raised his eyebrows, staring him down.

Andrew glared at him, his face warm. He felt embarrassed, as if it were him who had been caught behaving shamelessly in a public place.

"Tom, move to your own seat," the man said, pushing the redhead away gently. "We wouldn't want to offend anyone's sensibilities."

The redhead—Tom, apparently—whined. "Come on, Logan, just ignore the bigot," he grumbled, kissing him on the jaw. "He's been gawking at us since the airport."

Logan glanced at Andrew. "I know."

Flushing, Andrew looked away and glowered at the clouds outside the window.

Vivian cleared her throat. "I apologize for my husband," she said. "Andrew didn't mean any offense."

"I'm sure he didn't," Logan said, his voice very dry.

"No, really," Vivian said. "He's not bigoted. My brother is gay, too, and Andrew gets along with him just fine."

Andrew smiled a little, feeling a rush of fondness. Vivian was ever the peacemaker, but that was an exaggeration even by her standards.

He did get along with his brother-in-law, Derek Rutledge—if by "getting along" one meant that they tolerated each other for the good of the company and for the sake of Vivian.

They barely spoke to each other if it didn't concern Rutledge Enterprises, and Andrew talked to Derek's husband even less. He couldn't stand them, and it had nothing to do with him being bigoted. They had simply stolen everything he had worked for since he was twenty.

Sighing, Andrew reclined his seat back, closed his eyes, and tried to fall asleep. Sleep would help him pass the long flight from Tahiti back to the US, and it had the added benefit of preventing him from having to look at those people for hours. It had been a relaxing week, just the two of them in the beachside cabin they were staying in, but he felt so annoyed and tense now that he doubted he'd be able to fall asleep.

He must have managed to do it, because the next thing he knew, he was startled awake by a violent jolt.

For a moment, Andrew was disoriented, unsure where he was and what was happening.

Right. The plane.

The plane shuddered, again and again. They seemed to be caught in a thunderstorm, the clouds outside the window very dark, with lightning striking around them with alarming frequency.

The intercom chimed, followed by a tight female voice requesting all passengers to put their seats in the upright position and buckle down.

Doing as he was told, Andrew looked at Vivian in the seat next to him. She was very pale, her fingers gripping the armrest hard.

"Hey, it's normal," he said with a reassuring smile. "Turbulence. Every flight experiences some. Lightning can't hurt the plane." He tried not to think about the exceptions to the rule—the few cases when planes *had* crashed or been ripped apart due to bad storms.

Those cases were a statistical anomaly.

Vivian smiled back faintly and nodded.

A man raced past them in a hurry, some crew following him a few seconds later. Another bump in the air rattled the plane again, the trembles becoming more alarming. Someone in economy screamed.

Vivian reached out and grabbed his hand.

"We aren't crashing, don't be silly," Andrew said, squeezing it.

She didn't say anything, just looked at him with wide eyes full of terror.

Swallowing, Andrew took a deep breath. He knew he must remain calm for her sake—even if he was nervous, too.

"It's all right, honey," he said. "It will be all right—"

The plane convulsed harder and then *dropped,* and shrieks of terror filled the plane. They were now descending at an unforgiving speed. Vivian's hand clenched his so hard it was painful.

Biting the inside of his cheek, Andrew looked around the cabin, trying to distract himself from the fear on his wife's face.

His gaze locked with Logan's. The other man's eyes were grim, but his expression was calm and resolute. He didn't look afraid. Unlike him, his redheaded lover was crying in his seat, gripping his seatbelt and muttering something under his breath.

Oxygen masks fell from their compartments, and Andrew numbly helped Vivian to put it on before grabbing his.

He breathed and held his wife's hand, trying to remain calm.

For the first time in years, Andrew prayed.

Chapter 2

Logan groaned, hauling himself upright. His vision faded in and out, his body aching all over. He forced himself to focus.

The first thing he saw was Tom's body.

Logan didn't need to check Tom's pulse to know that he was dead. There was a gaping wound in Tom's head. Tom's blue eyes were lifeless, still wide with fear.

Bile rose in his throat. He had known Tom for just a few days, but it was still incredibly unsettling to see the guy he'd been kissing a few hours ago dead. Christ, Tom hadn't even been twenty-five yet.

Tearing his gaze away, Logan looked around. They were not losing altitude; that much was obvious. They'd landed, then. Crashed. It was light enough to see by, which meant that it was still day, wherever they'd landed. He tried to calculate just where they'd come down, based on the flight time, but came up blank. Okay; not important.

His gaze finally fell on the guy across the aisle. The guy—Andrew, if Logan remembered correctly—was crying, shaking his wife and begging her to wake up.

Logan stared at him, vaguely amazed by the transformation. Gone was the haughty, picture-perfect man sneering at him in contempt. This guy barely resembled him, his curly brown hair the only thing they had in common.

Shaking himself out of his stupor—had he hit his head?—Logan forced himself to move. He unbuckled his seatbelt and got to his feet, ignoring the dull pain in his ribs.

The plane was quiet. Too quiet. He had expected that there would be panic and people's screams, but there was nothing. When Logan parted the partition that separated the first-class cabin from economy class, he found out why: part of the plane was gone.

Logan glanced at the cloudy sky and then at the beach nearby. It seemed the plane—what was left of it— had crashed into the shallow waters of some island, far enough from the storm the plane had been caught in. Or perhaps it had been hours. How long had he been unconscious?

No locals. No houses anywhere to be seen. No sign that there was anyone but them on the island. Probably uninhabited, then. Wherever the other half of the plane was, he couldn't see it. It was possible it had already been swallowed by the ocean. Speaking of the ocean, it looked like the tide was coming in soon.

He returned inside and went to the cockpit. He didn't have much hope that anyone inside it was alive, and his expectations turned out to be correct when he found the bodies of the pilot and co-pilot.

Sighing, Logan carried them out of the plane, one by one, then carried out Tom's body. At last, there was only the bigot left. Him and his dead wife.

"Come on, carry her out," Logan said gruffly. "We can't leave the bodies here. The plane is going to flood when the tide comes."

The guy lifted his head and blinked at him dazedly. His wide eyes were very green.

Strange. Logan had thought they were blue.

He frowned and waved a hand in front of the guy's face. "Did you hit your head? Do you understand what I'm saying? Come on, the tide is starting to come in. There's no time to lose. Carry the body out."

"The body," the man repeated, looking lost. "She's—she isn't dead. She's just unconscious."

Logan looked away, his jaw clenching. He didn't want to feel sorry for that bigoted dick, but it was impossible not to. "She's dead," he said, a little softer, glancing at the unnatural angle of her neck. He pressed his fingers to her throat, just to be sure, and wasn't surprised not to find the pulse. "I'm sorry for your loss, but we have to move. You can't stay here. Carry her out."

He didn't wait for the guy to follow his instructions. There was no time to babysit him: judging by the height of the waves, they had very little time left. So Logan busied himself with getting the carry-on bags out of the plane, and then all the food and water he could find. He had no idea when rescue would come, so it was better to be prepared than not.

At some point, the other man must have moved, because he wasn't in the plane when Logan returned after putting the bags on a higher point of the beach.

Rubbing his aching ribs, Logan looked around the rapidly flooding plane, searching for anything that might be remotely useful. He grabbed a handful of blankets, pillows, and some tools, and glanced at the cockpit. The plane's communication system didn't seem to work. He could only hope the plane had sent a distress signal before crashing and that rescue would be coming soon.

The water had already reached his waist, so Logan left the plane, figuring he'd done all he could.

He deposited everything next to the bags and pulled out his phone. No signal, as expected. That would have been too easy.

Running a hand over his face, Logan sighed and turned toward the bodies. He hesitated. If they were rescued soon, burying the bodies would be pointless, but he didn't like the idea of leaving them unburied in such heat. So he went to work.

Digging three graves with rudimentary, limited tools proved to be long, exhausting work, and by the time he was done, Logan was sweating profusely, his bruised ribs aching. He pulled off his drenched shirt, washed it in the ocean, and left it to dry on a rock.

Then he grabbed a bottle of water and went in search of the other guy. As much as he didn't like that dick, he didn't want him to die of dehydration.

He found him around the bend of the island, by a tall palm tree. Andrew was kneeling in front of a shallow mound of sand. A grave. He was covered in sand, his hands dirty and bloodied.

Logan frowned. Had he dug the grave with his hands?

"Hey," he said. "You should get some water into you."

The guy didn't move, still hunched over the grave. He was breathing raggedly, his breath coming out in harsh gasps. Or sobs.

"Are you hurt?" Logan said, eyeing him with mixed feelings.

As much as he hated the thought of being stranded on some godforsaken island with a bigot, the guy had just lost his wife. A nice, lovely woman who had spent the flight trying to defend her homophobic husband.

If Logan remembered correctly, she had mentioned that they'd been married for nine years. Nine years with one person was a long time. Logan couldn't hope to understand the enormity of losing one's spouse of nine years. Although he did feel sad about Tom, they'd barely known each other. Tom was—had been—another tourist Logan had hooked up with on Bora Bora; it could hardly compare to losing one's wife.

There was no reaction.

Logan's lips thinned. He'd never exactly been known for his patience, and unfortunately for Andrew, he was too exhausted and stressed to make an effort now.

He dropped the bottle at Andrew's feet and strode away.

The guy was a grown man. He wasn't going to babysit him.

If he wanted to die of dehydration, it was his own choice.

***

Logan spent the next few days exploring the island.

Unfortunately, there wasn't much to explore. They were stranded on a tiny piece of land barely one square mile big. The island probably didn't even have a name. It probably wasn't on any maps, just one of thousands of small isles in the Pacific Ocean.

The only piece of good news was that there was fresh water: a tiny creek. The water tasted a little metallic but was good enough to drink. At least he hadn't been poisoned after drinking it.

There was no animal life, and no sign of humans ever being there.

In light of this, and considering that rescue still failed to appear, Logan spent a day making a fishing net from the clothes he'd found in Vivian's carry-on bag. He felt a little bad for destroying a dead woman's belongings, but he figured she wouldn't mind her clothes being used to feed her widower. It was only practical: out of all the clothes, hers weren't something they could wear—unless they got really desperate, but Logan tried not to think about that option. If they got desperate enough to need to wear Vivian's clothes, that would mean they would have been stranded on this island for a very, very long time.

He actually sort of wanted Andrew to get angry over his wife's clothes. The silence was starting to get on Logan's nerves. The guy walked around the island like some kind of ghost, his gaze listless and lost. He barely touched the water and food Logan left for him several times a day. He didn't speak at all. It was a stark contrast to the confrontational guy who had been glaring at him and Tom with disgust only a few days ago.

Something had to give; it couldn't go on like this.

Chapter 3

Andrew wanted to get drunk.

There was a bottle of vodka among the things Logan had salvaged from the plane. Andrew grabbed it when the other man wasn't looking, went to his wife's grave, and got smashingly drunk. It was a good feeling.

Logan found him a few hours later and was, quite predictably, furious. But then again, he seemed to have only two moods, as far as Andrew was concerned: disgusted and furious.

"Go away," Andrew slurred, looking up at him from the ground. "You're killing the mood here."

His voice sounded strange even to his own ears. Hoarse and croaky. How long had he not used it? Since…

Andrew took another swig from the bottle, relishing the burn.

He was pretty sure Logan's face would have turned red with rage had it not been already so sun-bronzed.

"I told you: you aren't allowed to take anything without my approval first," Logan gritted out, a muscle ticking at his temple.

Andrew snorted, kicking Logan's shin. It was a pity he was barefoot.

It probably didn't even hurt that asshole. "You're the biggest control freak I've ever met."

His lips twisted into a smile. "And I've known quite a few control freaks, so that actually says a lot. Are you sure you didn't attend Joseph Rutledge's school for the most controlling dicks on the planet?"

Logan shot him a disgusted look. "Get up. Drink some water and go sleep it off."

Andrew kicked him on the shin again. The asshole didn't even budge. "You aren't the boss of me."

"No," Logan said. "But I'm the guy in charge of the stash, not you. You don't get to take anything you like. Our supplies are limited—"

"It's just vodka. What use—"

"It was the only thing here that could be used as an antiseptic," Logan ground out. "And now we have nothing, thanks to you."

Oh.

Andrew looked back at the bottle.

There was a long, tense silence.

Andrew stared at the bottle's label. "It's her birthday today," he whispered, and then he laughed, the sound harsh and jarring even to his own ears. "I think. How fucked up is it that I don't even know for sure what day it is?"

A sigh.

"That's hardly a good reason to get wasted—"

"She thought she might be pregnant."

Silence.

Logan didn't say anything.

Andrew gulped down what was left in the bottle and looked at the sky as he fought the tightness in his throat. Fuck, he didn't know why he felt like this. It wasn't like he had wanted kids all that much: Vivian had been the one who wanted them so badly.

Andrew could still remember her wide smile and the tears in her eyes when she had realized that her period was late. She had decided to do a pregnancy test when they got back to the US, afraid of yet another disappointment. They had been trying for over six years, with Vivian getting more and more desperate as she approached forty. Was it ironic that she had died just as her dream was possibly about to come true? Ironic was the wrong word. Fucked up. Cruel. Fucking unfair and stupid.

And now he'd never even know if she really had been pregnant. He would always wonder.

"I'm sorry for your loss," Logan said, his voice gruff.

Andrew snorted. "Right. It's not like people like you would ever understand what it's like to lose a wife."

"People like me," Logan said flatly.

Andrew kicked the bottle toward the ocean. "Homos."

"Do you actually *want* to get the shit kicked out of you?"

Lifting his eyes, Andrew focused his gaze on Logan's pissed-off face and smiled. *Maybe I do*, he thought. Physical hurt to distract him from the pain in his chest sounded almost welcome. "Did I offend you? Aren't you a homo? A cocksucker? A faggot?"

Logan's lips pressed together, his brown eyes darkening. "I don't know what you're trying to accomplish, but you won't get a rise out of me with a few juvenile insults."

Andrew stretched his mouth into a sneer. "I just can't help but notice that you didn't even shed a tear for your boyfriend—or whatever that guy who was all over you was. But then again, I've always known homos didn't give a shit about anything but sticking their dicks into other homos. You wouldn't understand things like love and grief—" He yelped as Logan hauled him to his feet roughly.

"One more word, and I'll fucking punch you," Logan said, his fingers digging painfully into Andrew's shoulders. "I gave you a lot of slack, because you're grieving and all, but I'm really getting fed up with your bigoted bullshit." He shook him like a ragdoll. "This is your last warning."

Andrew swallowed, his heart beating so fast it felt like it was trying to escape his chest.

Logan was big. It was a stupid thing to notice, but he'd never been this close to him before. Logan was big. The weird thing was, he didn't look all that big from afar— maybe because he was tall and muscular without much fat—but this close, it was obvious that the guy was built like a tank. He towered over Andrew by more than half a head, and Andrew wasn't exactly short, either—five foot eleven. It wasn't just the height or the muscular build. The guy's presence was oppressively strong, his dark gaze heavy and hostile. Coupled with his dark scruff and grumpy disposition, he looked uncannily like Wolverine, which was amusing, considering his name. Or would have been amusing if Andrew were capable of feeling amusement anymore.

Andrew heard himself say, "Get your disgusting hands off me."

The punch to his gut wasn't surprising, but the force of it sent him to his knees.

He laughed. "Am I supposed to be scared, you homo?"

Logan buried a hand in his hair and yanked his head up, forcing him to look at him. "You bigoted little dick—" He cut himself off, just looking at him intently. Studying him.

It made Andrew feel uncomfortable. Transparent. As if the other man could see right into his soul.

At last, Logan heaved a sigh, the anger and tension leaving his body. He ran a hand over his face and then looked Andrew in the eyes. "Look," he said. "I'm really sorry for your loss. But get it together. This… self-destructive behavior is fucking unhealthy. Get a goddamn grip. I'm sure your wife wouldn't have wanted you to get into fights you can't win or drink yourself into an early grave. She seemed like a smart woman. Kind. But she's gone. You're not."

Andrew's vision was suddenly blurry.

She seemed like a smart woman. Kind. But she's gone.

He didn't know why those words hit him so hard. It wasn't like he hadn't known Vivian was dead—he'd buried her with his own hands—but somehow, those words, uttered by a near stranger, made it real. She was gone. She really was gone. Gone. Dead. He'd never see her again.

A lump formed in Andrew's throat, his vision getting blurrier. He blinked rapidly, hating himself for showing weakness in front of this man, but he couldn't stop. He couldn't hold back the tears.

He turned his face away, trying to hide them, his breath coming out in ragged gasps.

Logan was mercifully quiet.

But he hadn't left.

Andrew hoped the sound of the waves crashing against the shore masked his ragged breathing, but knowing his luck, it probably didn't.

Logan remained silent for a while, allowing him to get a grip on his emotions while both of them pretended that he wasn't crying.

God, how fucking humiliating.

At long last, Logan cleared his throat. "Come on, get up," he said, his voice gruff. "We need to hydrate you."

Andrew looked at him, telling himself he *wasn't* embarrassed by the tears in his eyes. His wife was dead. He had every right to grieve her, dammit.

"Why do you care?" he whispered.

Logan's expression was somewhat pinched. "I don't. But I'll be damned if I have to dig another grave."

Despite his harsh words, his dark eyes weren't unkind as he offered his hand. "Get up, come on."

Andrew stared at that hand for a moment. Finally, he accepted it and allowed Logan to pull him up to his feet.

His knees were shaky, and the world around him wasn't quite in focus, but Logan caught him when he stumbled.

It felt symbolic, somehow.

Chapter 4

Days dragged by.

Logan had explored the small island completely, so now he had nothing to do but watch the empty horizon.

It was mind-numbingly boring. Back home, business kept him so busy that Logan had had little time for sleep, and he wasn't used to doing nothing.

At least the other inhabitant of the island was providing a break from the boredom. After their confrontation on the beach, Andrew had been... better. The guy still mostly kept to himself, but at least he no longer walked around like a ghost. He no longer tried to provoke Logan into beating him up. He started eating with Logan, though he threw tantrums for some inane reason a few times a day before storming off to sulk like an overgrown child. Apparently it wasn't enough that Andrew was a bigot; he was also a whiner. He whined and bitched about pretty much everything, but Logan didn't mind.

It was almost a relief. Confrontational was better than depressed. Not to mention that Andrew's hissy fits were somewhat entertaining, and entertainment was sorely lacking on the island. Their laptops' batteries had died ages ago, as did their phones and powerbanks, so Logan found himself growing increasingly restless, almost looking forward to the inevitable confrontation every day.

"I'm sick of fish," Andrew said with resentment, looking at the fish on his plate. "It's barely edible."

Logan leaned against the palm trunk and picked at his fish. It was a little burned, as it always was. The fish were plentiful around the island but small and bony. And bland. "I've never claimed to be a culinary genius. I'm a businessman, not a boy scout. If you don't like it, feel free to cook yourself. Feed yourself. An alien concept, isn't it?"

Andrew shot him a baleful look, pouting fiercely. He was the only person of Logan's acquaintance who managed to *pout* fiercely. It was bizarre. It also made him want to shove something into that pouty mouth, just to shut him up.

Right. Anyway.

"How old even are you?" Logan said. "You'd make a five-year-old proud with your tantrums."

Andrew glared at him. "I'll have you know I'm thirty-two."

Logan stared at him, genuinely surprised. Andrew didn't look like he was in his thirties. His skin still had the healthy glow of youth, perfect and smooth, not a wrinkle on his face. He looked great. Logan was annoyed with himself for even noticing it, but he was a healthy gay man with functional eyes, and Andrew was a very attractive guy, with a toned, surfer's body, a handsome face, and plump, pretty lips that were practically begging for—

"You look younger," Logan said, averting his gaze. "I thought your wife must have robbed the cradle."

Andrew's expression shuttered. "She's—was eight years older than me," he said, his voice toneless, and then walked away. Not sulking this time. Just sad.

***

It was the evening of their twenty-first day on the island when Andrew said, "No one is coming, right?"

Logan lifted his gaze from his fish—frankly, at this point, he was as sick of fish as Andrew was—and met the other man's eyes.

They stared at each other over the fire as the crickets chirped in the night.

No one is coming.

That was something he'd been trying hard not to think about, but it was undeniable that it should have taken people less time to find them. Maybe something had gone wrong with the plane's communication system and the search and rescue teams had no idea where to look. The Pacific Ocean was enormous, and who knew how much the storm had altered the plane's flight path?

Or perhaps they had found the other part of the plane—it seemed as though the plane had been ripped apart high in the air. It was possible that the other wreckage had ended up a great distance from where they currently were and had already been found—and people had stopped searching, thinking them all dead.

Logan turned away from Andrew and walked to their dwindling supplies.

His gaze stopped on the piece of cloth that held what he'd been carefully avoiding thinking about: the tomato seeds he'd saved from the sole tomato he'd grabbed from the plane.

He unwrapped the cloth and stared at the tiny seeds, his stomach twisted into an uncomfortable knot.

He'd saved them just in case. He hadn't really thought they would ever need them.

"There's still a chance," Logan heard himself say, putting the seeds back. "Even if they stop searching for us, maybe some ship will pass close enough to see us." His words sounded unconvincing, even to his own ears. In the three weeks they'd been stuck there, they hadn't seen a single ship, not even from a distance. The island was clearly away from usual ship routes.

Andrew's jaw clenched. He gave a clipped nod and averted his gaze.

It was the first time Andrew didn't take his blanket to sleep at the other end of the island. He stretched out just a few feet away and closed his eyes.

After extinguishing the fire, Logan lay down on his own blanket. Shoving his pillow under his head, he gazed at the night sky. The stars glittered prettily overhead, and he thought about how deceiving some impressions were. The stars were billions of miles apart from each other, no matter how close they appeared in the sky.

He couldn't fall asleep for a long time, and he knew Andrew wasn't asleep, either.

Neither of them said anything.

There was nothing to say.

No one is coming, right?

He would plant the seeds tomorrow.

Chapter 5

Logan snapped his eyes open and stared into the darkness, unsure what had woken him up.

There. A sniffle, muffled but audible.

Logan closed his eyes and tried to ignore it. It was none of his business. It wasn't his job to comfort the guy.

Another sniffle.

"Shut up," Logan said with a sigh.

Silence.

"Fuck you," Andrew said finally, but his voice sounded too thick to be convincing. Small. He sounded small.

Logan opened his eyes again, suppressing the urge to swear. He was not in the mood to deal with this. He just wanted to sleep. He wanted Andrew to keep acting like the bigoted little shit he was, not sound like he needed a hug.

"Why are you crying?" Logan said. His voice didn't come out as annoyed as he thought he was.

There was a long silence.

His eyelids started becoming heavier again by the time Andrew spoke.

"Do you have anyone missing you back home?"

Logan stared at the stars overhead. "I have a mother and two younger sisters. Dozens of annoying but well-meaning cousins. Friends." He hesitated before asking, "You?"

Andrew didn't answer.

***

It became something of a habit.

Suddenly, Andrew wanted to *talk*. It never happened during the day, only under the cover of the night. He asked about Logan's family, about where he'd gone to school, what he did for a living—

"Really? You don't look like a hotel owner."

Strictly speaking, it was a hotel chain rather than a hotel, but Logan didn't correct him. "What's with the sudden interest?"

"I'm bored."

This Logan could relate to. There was only so much time one could spend alone with one's thoughts without going crazy.

"What about you?" he asked when the silence stretched. "What do you do for a living?"

"I'm the CEO of Rutledge Enterprises."

Logan hummed, a little surprised. He had thought the guy must have been a trust-fund baby—but then again, he could well be. "Family company?"

Andrew snorted. "It belonged to Vivian's father, but the old bastard was still stuck in the nineteenth century and left the majority of the company to his son. Misogynistic ass. Vivian got just ten percent of the company's shares."

There was a great deal of bitterness in Andrew's voice, but to Logan's surprise and relief, he no longer sounded wretched every time his wife was mentioned. Maybe he was finally moving on from his grief. Good. A moping Andrew was insufferable. More insufferable than he normally was.

"Sore subject?" Logan said.

Andrew laughed. "I've slaved for that company since I was twenty, but apparently leaving the company to a son who knows nothing about the business made more sense than leaving it to someone who actually knows how to manage it."

"Aren't you the CEO?"

"Yes, but I still answer to Derek Rutledge. It's not the same."

Logan did the math in his head.

So Andrew worked for the company since he was twenty. If he and his wife had been married for nine years…

"So you married the boss's daughter?"

He could feel Andrew's glare on him even despite the dark. "If you're implying I married her in order to get promoted—"

"Not implying anything."

After a lengthy silence, Andrew sighed. "I guess she did attract my attention because she was the boss's daughter, but it became more than that soon enough." His tone turned wistful, softer. "She was… She was so lovely and kind and…"

He trailed off, but Logan could guess what he meant. He hadn't really thought the guy was a fortune hunter. His affection for his wife had clearly been genuine; Logan would him give that.

"Everyone still thought I was a fortune hunter," Andrew said, as if reading his thoughts. He chuckled. "I was a nobody, and she was an heiress of one of the richest families in the country. The old Rutledge despised me but had to tolerate me, because he'd already lost his only son over his choice of bed partners, and he couldn't afford to lose his only daughter over her choice of a husband."

Logan made a face. He knew men like that: old money, too set in their old ways. He could only imagine how a pompous ass like that would react to getting an upstart for a son-in-law. It almost made him feel sorry for Andrew. Almost. Sucking up to such an asshole of a father-in-law for years and in the end not even inheriting the family company would have made anyone pissed off and bitter.

"Now you being a dick makes a little bit more sense," Logan said wryly. "A little bit."

"Fuck off," Andrew said, but it lacked any heat. He always was quieter at night. Not as brash as he was during the day. More like a person.

It was… unsettling. Logan actually preferred the obnoxious dick he'd first met. He knew how to deal with the spiteful little bigot Andrew was ninety percent of the time. This quiet, lonely guy was another matter entirely.

It messed with Logan's head. Coupled with the looks Andrew had been giving him lately, it had the potential for disaster.

***

They ran out of matches on the forty-sixth day.

"What are we going to do?" Andrew said, his voice cracking a little.

Logan looked at him. Sometimes he marveled over how much the guy had changed over the past month and a half. It wasn't that Andrew had suddenly become a nice human being. No. He was still whiny and bitchy, and he still kept dropping snide remarks from time to time, but gone was the arrogant man who'd sneered at him from across the aisle.

Those large, blue-green eyes were full of fear and uncertainty now—and something that looked an awful lot like the need for reassurance.

Why are you looking at me like this, damn you?

"We'll try starting a fire without matches," Logan said, turning away so he didn't have to look into those uncertain eyes.

"Right," Andrew said. "If cavemen could do it, surely it isn't that difficult, right?"

Fuck, he really was seeking reassurance from him.

Grimacing, Logan ran a hand over his scruffy face.

"Right," he said gruffly. "Let's get on with it."

***

Creating fire without matches was easier said than done.

Even if they managed to get a spark, making fire out of that spark was another matter entirely. Dry firewood was sparse—the island's micro-climate was too humid. On the rare occasion that they got the fire going, sudden showers could destroy all their efforts. It didn't help that there were no caves on the island, nothing that could serve as a natural shelter from rain.

As a result, they often were hungry, annoyed, and soaked—not a good combination when they could barely stand each other.

They'd had so many shouting matches these days, a mere glance from Andrew could work him up. Logan wasn't proud of himself, but it was what it was. He knew they were just lashing out, needing an outlet for their ever-growing frustration and fear, but it did nothing to alleviate those emotions.

With every passing day, the tiny hope that rescue was coming became smaller and smaller until it finally shriveled up and died.

No one was coming.

They were likely going to be stuck on this island for the rest of their lives.

The thought was difficult to accept, but eventually, Logan did accept it.

He had no idea what was going on in Andrew's head—if he accepted it, too—but the guy had started seeking him out more often, for some stupid confrontation about everything and nothing. It didn't seem to matter what they were fighting about; Andrew still stuck close to him. And Logan… He didn't tell him to get lost. Couldn't bring himself to do it.

Rationally, Logan understood what was going on. Humans were social creatures. They couldn't survive on their own, without interacting with other humans. Even the most introverted people needed company once in a while, especially when they were stuck on a tiny island with nothing to do to pass the time.

It was just a base need for company. That was all it was. It didn't mean Logan suddenly liked that bigoted dick, no matter how pleadingly he looked at him lately. If anything, those looks just annoyed him. *Tell me we'll be rescued. Tell me we'll be okay. Tell me we won't die here. Look at me, tell me, look at me.*

It pissed Logan off. He'd never liked neediness, never wanted anyone to need him.

And yet here he was, tolerating those looks and those petty squabbles over nothing—because he needed them, too. Months with nothing but his own thoughts, without any purpose, were starting to drive him crazy.

That was the only explanation for why Andrew's needy behavior didn't irritate him as much as it should have.

It still creeped him out—because part of him was starting to *like* being needed.

***

The need for social interaction he could tolerate.

The *touching* that started a few weeks after that was far more unsettling.

It started with small things. Andrew's shoulder would sometimes bump against his. Andrew's hand would brush against his as they worked together on building a shelter. Andrew would shove him when he was annoyed, his fingers splaying over Logan's bare chest.

At first Logan wrote those things off as accidents. But they kept happening, so he started observing the other man. The touches… they didn't seem to be conscious on Andrew's part. Andrew was still being his prickly, hostile self, mostly, but his body seemed to gravitate closer to Logan.

It made sense, probably. Just like with the need for social interaction, humans were tactile by nature. From infancy, they craved the touch of another being. They didn't do well without touching and being touched by others. He and Andrew had been stranded on this small piece of land for nearly three months now. It was probably natural that after so long in such isolation, they would start needing the reassurance of human contact.

Now that Logan was paying attention, he caught himself standing closer to the other guy than was strictly necessary, too.

His self-control was still better than Andrew's, but he wasn't sure how long it would last, to be honest. The loneliness and the empty years that stretched ahead of them ate at him, too, and as the weeks turned into months, he'd started forgetting why this was a bad idea. If they were never going to return to civilization, what was the harm in taking what little comfort another person's touch brought?

So when Andrew's bare arm brushed against his, Logan didn't push him away. When Andrew slumped against him, sweaty and exhausted after they'd finishing building the shelter, Logan allowed it, looking at the sun disappearing into the ocean. The right side of his body, where Andrew was pressed against him, was tingling. Andrew's shoulder was warm and solid, and sitting like this was… It wasn't unpleasant.

But it also put him on edge, his cock hard and fat in his shorts. He ignored it. He'd become good at ignoring it. Spending so much time around a half-naked, ridiculously hot guy would make any gay man horny, especially considering that he hadn't gotten laid in months. His cock didn't seem to care what a bad idea it was. Nor did it care that the guy was a bigot. It was just a natural physical response, and Logan had been ignoring it for months now. But with every day, his reservations seemed to fade away, and it was becoming more difficult to suppress his body's needs.

Fuck, he'd never been so frustrated.

Logan pressed the heel of his hand to his cock through his shorts. At this point, he didn't give a damn if Andrew saw him doing it. Some bigoted, disgusting nonsense would actually be welcome right now, to help him deal with the inappropriate arousal.

Being reminded of what a piece of shit Andrew was would surely help him kill his erection. But if Andrew noticed, he didn't say anything. His eyes were half-closed, exhaustion and sleepiness etched into his lovely features.

Lovely. Logan was kind of disgusted with himself for even thinking that word, but it really fit. Andrew's features were unbelievably lovely, the orange rays of the evening sun illuminating his sun-kissed face, the tiny freckles on his cheekbones, his long, dark eyelashes, and his plump, slightly parted lips.

Logan wrenched his eyes away. Tried to remember what a homophobic little shit Andrew was. He did remember. His cock didn't care.

"You think the shelter will keep the rain out?" Andrew said, without opening his eyes.

Logan hummed noncommittally, glancing at the dark clouds to the west. If the wind was any indication, they were going to find out soon enough. They'd become rather good at recognizing the telltale signs of showers.

"Hope it works," Andrew murmured. "I hate being wet." His finger traced Logan's knee absentmindedly.

Logan gritted his teeth. He got to his feet, dumping the guy off his shoulder unceremoniously.

"Dick," Andrew said, glaring at him sleepily. It wasn't attractive at all.

Logan turned away. "We need to gather firewood before the rain hits, or we'll go hungry for days. Go."

Andrew grumbled something but didn't really argue. Paradoxically, Logan had found that the guy rarely protested if Logan phrased his suggestions as an order. It was when Logan asked for Andrew's opinion that they would argue until they were blue in the face.

It made Logan wonder.

Chapter 6

It started raining the next morning, as expected.

They hid in their shelter, the fire crackling merrily in the corner as they ate their meager meal. The sound of the rain beating against the ground, splashing against puddles and the ocean, pervaded the air.

It would almost be cozy if Andrew weren't so acutely aware of Logan's body beside his.

The shelter was small. It was just big enough for them to sit comfortably, and the dining area with the improvised fireplace took a good part of it, leaving very little space for them to sleep. They'd tried to make the shelter bigger, but the structure had become unbalanced, so they'd had to settle for an enclosure that was barely big enough for two grown men. As a result, they had to put their bedding side by side, with next to no space between them.

After extinguishing the fire, Andrew lay down on his side, on the very edge of his blanket, as far from Logan as possible, which wasn't very far. Above them, the rain was hammering down onto the roof, making the space feel more intimate and closed in, as though they were being held together in a warm, careful hand.

Goddammit. He hoped it wouldn't rain for days again.

He could feel Logan behind him.

Andrew had always thought it was ridiculous when people said they could sense someone's presence without looking, but now he knew it wasn't an exaggeration. He could—could sense it with his own skin. Logan always seemed to run hot, his large body like a fucking furnace. It was annoying. It was uncomfortable. The heat was unbearable as it was. Andrew would never get used to the island's micro-climate: it was too hot despite raining half of the time, the moisture preserving the heat and making it hard to breathe sometimes.

Since they usually avoided ruining their limited clothes with sweat, they both were wearing just a pair of shorts—and Andrew had never been more aware of it. He was used to Logan walking around half-naked, but this was different.

He was in a tiny space with a gay man, and they both were nearly naked.

Andrew's stomach clenched. He'd seen the outline of Logan's hard dick yesterday. Logan seemed perpetually hard lately. Andrew had done his best to pretend that he hadn't noticed anything, but he had. Of course he fucking had. He had functional eyes, and there was nothing to look at on this island besides Logan.

He was in a very small shelter with a half-naked, horny gay man.

What if…

What if Logan was finally going to molest him? Would he do it while Andrew slept?

Andrew swallowed as he imagined Logan pressing his body against his and groping his body in his sleep. Molesting him. Groping Andrew's cock. Stroking his nipples. Groping his ass. Pushing his hard cock against Andrew's ass while Andrew was none the wiser.

The perv would probably pull Andrew's shorts down and rub his stiff cock between his cheeks, grunting like an animal and taking his pleasure while Andrew slept peacefully, unaware that he was being violated.

Would he wake up? Or would he keep sleeping? Maybe if Logan was really careful, Andrew wouldn't even find out about it until the morning when he'd find dried come on his ass. Or maybe he would wake up, but Logan wouldn't stop, forcing him to be still as he thrust his cock between Andrew's thighs. Logan was bigger and stronger than he was. Andrew wouldn't be able to stop him. Logan could do whatever he wanted to him, and Andrew wouldn't be able to do anything about it. Logan might force him to suck his cock, which would be disgusting, but Andrew would have to do it; he'd have no choice.

A small sound snapped him out of his thoughts.

It took Andrew a moment to realize that he was the one who'd made the sound.

"If you're going to jerk off, go do it outside," Logan said.

Andrew flushed. What—

Wait, his hand was palming his cock through his shorts.

Andrew frowned, unsure when it had even happened. He was hard, for no reason. Well, it had been months since the last time he'd gotten off, and it probably made sense that his libido was returning. He was a healthy man in the prime of his life. His body had needs, and it didn't care that this was the unsexiest situation he'd ever been in and that mentally he wasn't exactly in the mood.

"I'm not going outside when it's pouring," he said in his most confident, contrary tone. Offense was the best defense, after all. "I'll jerk off wherever I damn please."

Behind him, Logan breathed out through his gritted teeth—at least it sounded like it. Andrew could practically see it: the way Logan's firm jaw clenched, his dark eyes glowering at the back of Andrew's head.

"Don't you have any shame?"

Andrew's face was warm. He hadn't exactly intended to jerk off in Logan's presence, but it wasn't like he could backtrack now without making it look like he was doing as Logan said.

"It's a natural physical need," Andrew said in his most nonchalant voice as he palmed his cock. "Close your eyes and stop eavesdropping, you perv."

Logan laughed harshly. "It's not eavesdropping when it's happening right here."

"Does it really bother you? That's rich coming from a guy who didn't mind another guy groping him on a plane."

Logan had nothing to say to that, and Andrew smiled, pleased that he'd had the last word. He pulled his shorts down and nearly gasped as his hand finally closed around his erection. Fuck, it felt good. He'd forgotten that he could feel good at all.

Biting his bottom lip to keep himself from making any sounds, Andrew started stroking his cock, acutely aware of the other man's body behind him. The rain drummed outside, and the primitive sound somehow just made him hornier. To his surprise, he didn't feel embarrassed at all. Maybe he'd just gotten used to Logan always being around lately. Maybe he was just out of fucks to give. Or maybe he wanted to annoy the hell out of Logan. It didn't matter. It felt good.

He turned onto his back and started stroking himself faster, his pre-come making it easier, the slick sound of a hand moving on a cock unmistakable in the silence.

He kept his eyes shut, but he could feel Logan to his right, could hear his harsh breathing.

"I could fucking strangle you right now," Logan bit off.

A thrill shot through his body. Andrew moaned, quickening his strokes. "Keep your sick fantasies to yourself," he said breathlessly.

"You're such a little shit," Logan said, sounding pissed. There was some rustling, and then there was the sound of flesh moving against flesh.

Andrew's eyes snapped open.

It was too dark in the shelter to see anything clearly, but he could make out Logan's hand moving…

Fuck.

Andrew slammed his eyes shut. It didn't matter. He didn't actually see anything. He could pretend it wasn't happening—that Logan wasn't stroking his cock a few inches away from him.

Gross. The mere idea… of Logan's large hand fisting that fat cock—it was disgusting. Utterly disgusting. Positively sickening.

Another moan left his lips, his hand working his cock faster.

"Shut up," Logan said gruffly.

Andrew scowled. Just to be contrary, he became louder, allowing himself to make noises. Screw Logan. Screw him. Ugh, he couldn't stand him. He hated him so much.

What a fucking hypocrite. He'd berated Andrew for being shameless, but now he was getting himself off, probably imagining shutting him up with his cock— stuffing that thick cock into Andrew's mouth and forcing him to gag on it, choke on his jizz and—

The orgasm caught him off guard. Andrew moaned, stroking himself through it until he became oversensitive.

He panted, his other hand running all over his chest and arm, trying to comfort himself and not crash too hard. He'd always liked being held after sex. It had actually been the favorite part of his sex life with Vivian. She was—had been—amazing at making him feel good afterward. God, he missed her. She would have hugged him and stroked his hair, she would have told him how good he had been for her. She would have—

Hot tears sprang to his eyes.

Christ, he couldn't believe she was dead. Couldn't believe she would never put her arms around him and hold him against her soft chest.

A low grunt snapped him to the present. Andrew flushed in discomfort, realizing that Logan must have come, too. There was silence in the shelter now, broken only by the sound of the rain outside.

Was it his imagination or was the rain really letting up?

God, he could only hope.

Chapter 7

The rain didn't let up.

He and Logan had been stuck inside the shelter for three days now, and it was driving Andrew crazy.

The close quarters would have been okay—they had learned to co-exist in the past months, and Andrew had to admit even Logan's company was better than being on his own—but ever since that first night…

Putting it bluntly, he was horny as hell.

It seemed that now that his body remembered that it had *needs*, it decided to keep reminding him of it all the time. It was beyond inconvenient. And a little embarrassing.

Though maybe it should have been more embarrassing than it was. Maybe he should have been more weirded out by the fact that every night he jerked off next to a practically naked, horny gay man.

But truth be told, Andrew had become used to Logan always being around. He didn't even like the guy, but… having him around was sort of comforting. No, "comforting" was the wrong word. There was nothing comforting about Logan: the guy was a moody, grumpy dick who clearly barely tolerated him. But lately, *not* having him around put Andrew on edge. Off balance. The loneliness, the lack of purpose and meaning in this life… it ate at him, every day.

He sometimes thought he hated Logan, but he hated being alone with his thoughts—being alone, period—even more.

When Logan was around, the world came a little more into focus. Andrew knew it wasn't normal, knew that it was some kind of weird dependency born out of loneliness and desperation, but he could do nothing about it.

He didn't want to be alone.

They did everything together these days: cooked, scavenged, argued—and just sat in silence. Silence with Logan around didn't feel as daunting and scary as the silence when Andrew was alone.

Maybe that was why jerking off with Logan around didn't feel anywhere near as weird as it should have been—*would* have been in the real world. In this strange, surreal world where only the two of them existed, it was just another thing they did together.

But while he might not have been all that weirded out about the whole thing, it didn't mean he wasn't aware that Logan might not be as blasé about it as he was.

Logan wasn't straight. Unlike Andrew, he loved cock. He loved sticking his cock into other men. So really, getting off beside Logan was… probably not ideal. A little reckless. As provocative as a hot, naked woman getting herself off next to Andrew every night would have been.

Andrew wasn't blind. He could sense the tension in Logan, the ever-growing frustration, could see the way the other man's cock would get hard several times a day. Um, he wasn't *staring* at the guy's crotch all the time or anything; it was just right there. Anyone would look. Anyone would notice, considering how fucking big that thing was.

Coupled with the fact that the guy couldn't stand him, it seemed it was only a matter of time before Logan finally snapped. So Andrew should probably stop doing this next to him.

But fuck, he couldn't. He liked—needed—to feel good. And this was pretty much the only way he could feel good on this godforsaken island where nothing ever happened. The mind-numbing dullness of this existence was driving him crazy—he felt like he was slowly losing his mind—and he wasn't about to deprive himself of this small comfort. Even his own touch was better than nothing.

So he ignored Logan and touched himself.

If Logan got any ideas, Andrew would simply tell him to keep his paws off him.

***

It happened on the fourth day of continuous rain.

Andrew was curled up on his side, his back to Logan, his hand working leisurely on his cock. His shorts were kicked off to his feet, because he hated how restricted he felt in them. It was dark in the shelter, so it didn't matter anyway. Logan couldn't see him.

He stroked his cock slowly to the drum of the rain outside. Cap-cap, cap-cap, cap-cap.

He wondered dazedly if this was what the primitive humans used to do all the time: with no Internet and no entertainment to pass the time, they had probably just touched their cocks all day long. Maybe they had public orgies all the time, going around naked, breasts and cocks on display. Naked, pretty women sucking thick, hard cocks… red cockheads glistening with pre-come… Mmm… Though there were probably homos back then, too.

The mental image of cavemen sucking each other's cocks was… obviously nowhere near as appealing as perky breasts.

"Do you think there were gay Neanderthals?"

Fuck. His brain-to-mouth filter seemed non-existent lately.

"Are you serious?" Logan's voice was a little strangled, amusement mixed with annoyance. "What kind of question is that?"

"Just had a thought," Andrew said, still stroking his cock lazily.

"Your brain is a very weird place."

Andrew hummed noncommittally.

"Why are you thinking about gay cavemen while you're jacking off?" Logan said.

"How do you know I'm jacking off?"

"I have ears."

Andrew let go of his cock and brought his hand up his body, stroking his trembling stomach, and then kneading his pecs. His skin prickled, oversensitive after not being touched for so long. He moaned.

"Shut the fuck up," Logan said.

Andrew returned his hand to his cock. "No one forces you to listen."

"If I didn't know better, I'd think you were asking for it." Oh, Logan sounded *pissed*.

Andrew squeezed his cock, his arousal spiking. "I'm not responsible for your sick mind, you perv."

Logan laughed. "My sick mind? You're getting yourself off a few inches away from me and moaning like a porn star."

"It's not like you don't do it, too," Andrew said, stroking his cock faster.

"Everyone does it. It's a natural body function. Don't know why you're making such a big deal out of it."

"Already forgot that I'm a 'homo'?" Logan said scathingly.

Andrew bit his bottom lip. "Are you saying you can't control yourself? That's pretty pathetic."

"I can control myself," Logan said. "You aren't that hot. But shutting you up with my cock has never been more tempting."

Andrew licked the inside of his mouth, his heart hammering in his chest. He stroked his cock faster, painfully aware of Logan's large body behind his. "I told you to spare me your sick fantasies."

Logan laughed. "At least have the decency to stop jerking off while you're talking to me."

"Why? I'm perfectly capable of multitasking." In all honesty, he probably should stop talking to Logan, but Logan's low, growly voice—the danger of him snapping—it only made his pleasure sharper. He couldn't stop touching his cock, his hand flying faster over it, the slick sound of flesh against flesh filling the small shelter. He moaned—

Growling, Logan rolled and pressed himself flush against Andrew's back.

His very naked back.

"Get away from me, you—"

"Drop the act," Logan snapped, his hand gripping Andrew's hip. "You wouldn't be naked if you didn't want this, you bigoted little cocktease."

"I'm not a—"

"You're the biggest fucking cocktease I've ever met," Logan growled. "You go around half-naked, you jerk off next to me, you give me those needy doe eyes—"

"I don't!"

"You do. And you touch me all the time," Logan said and ground his cock between Andrew's cheeks.

His very hard cock.

Andrew had another man's cock rubbing against his ass.

God, it was so degrading. He was a man. A normal man. How dare that asshole rub his cock against him as if Andrew were a woman or a cock-hungry faggot? Andrew wanted to stop him. He did. But Logan was so much bigger and stronger than him. Fighting him would be pointless, right?

"So now you have to lie in the bed you made," Logan said, his breath hot and moist against Andrew's ear. "I'm finally doing what you wanted."

"I don't want this, you—you molester!"

Logan laughed, the sound low and full of amusement. "Molester? Why are you still jerking off, then?"

Andrew flushed, realizing that he *was* still stroking his cock. "I'm just horny," he said, defensively. "I was close to coming when you started molesting me. That's all."

"Don't stop on my account," Logan said, his tone very dry, as if he wasn't rutting between Andrew's cheeks like a disgusting animal. "Go on."

Andrew scowled, but fuck, he really was horny.

He wanted to get off.

Even having a naked man pressed so tightly against his back wasn't turning him off.

He blamed his touch starvation.

His skin was tingling at every point they were touching, and it was so hard to think about anything else. It felt so good. He needed to…

"Fine," he grumbled, resuming stroking. "But don't get any funny ideas. If you even think about sticking your cock in my ass—"

"Not planning to," Logan said. "I have standards."

"I *hate* you," Andrew said with feeling, fisting his cock faster. "God, I can't stand you."

Logan snorted. "The feeling is mutual, you bigoted little tease," he said, his cock pressing harder and harder between Andrew's cheeks.

The slippery head caught against his hole for a moment, and Andrew jerked, as if electrocuted, a hiss leaving his lips. "Don't you dare," he bit out, squeezing his own cock. "If you even think about sticking your huge, disgusting cock into my ass—"

"For a straight guy, you sure fixate on my cock's size a lot."

"Fuck you. My point is, if you even think about putting your cock in me, I swear I'll—I'll—"

"You what?" Logan said into his ear, his voice low and hoarse. "What will you do? Call the police? I can do anything to you, and no one will stop me."

"You're sick," Andrew moaned out, his hand slippery with pre-come as he jacked his cock faster.

"If I'm sick, so are you. It turns you on, you hypocrite." Logan bit his earlobe, making Andrew cry out. "You want me to force you. If I force you, it's not your fault, right? Is that how you think?"

"Shut up," Andrew muttered, his head spinning. He couldn't think, his whole world narrowed to his aching cock and balls—and to the cock rutting between his cheeks.

The obscene sound of flesh grinding against flesh, Logan's hot breath against his ear, his large, hard body against him...

It all did strange things to him, making him unable to form coherent thoughts.

It was probably the touch deprivation. After months of not being touched, having so much naked skin against his was *maddening*. Fuck, he shouldn't have been allowing this to happen—it was wrong and disgusting and depraved—but he couldn't fucking think. He was being forced, right? It wasn't his fault.

Moaning, he turned onto his belly, his erection trapped between his bedding and his stomach. Logan followed him, teeth sinking into his shoulder as his heavy body pressed him down, his hips thrusting, his cock sliding between Andrew's cheeks, harder and harder—

Andrew's orgasm was ripped out of him, a low groan leaving his mouth as he spilled onto his bedding.

He went boneless, his head blissfully empty for a while—until he felt the hot sticky liquid between his cheeks before Logan's heavy body went still on top of him.

"Ugh," Andrew said. "Get off me, that's disgusting!"

Logan rolled off him and lay on his back, still breathing hard.

Andrew panted into his thin pillow, dread, panic, and mortification filling his chest as the fog of pleasure faded. Fuck. What had they done?

"It isn't happening again," he said shakily.

"Whatever," Logan said, his tone clipped. He sounded pissed. But then again, he always sounded pissed.

Andrew shifted and grimaced at the sticky mess under him and on him. He didn't want to lie on the wet spot.

"Give me your bed," he said, sitting up and wiping his ass against his bedding. It was ruined anyway.

"Fuck off."

"It's your fault mine is ruined!"

Logan groaned. "You're so damn annoying. Fuck off. I'm not sleeping on your jizz."

Andrew glowered at him in the dark. "I'm not sleeping on it, either!"

Yawning, Logan chuckled. "You're welcome to try to move me."

"Ugh!" Andrew kicked him on the shin. "If you're as inconsiderate of your fucktoys, no wonder you can't keep any relationships."

"Whatever gave you that idea?" The asshole sounded sleepy and a little curious.

Andrew scoffed. "Please. You're almost thirty-four, rich, and not entirely ugly—"

"Thanks," Logan said dryly.

"You wouldn't still be picking up pretty boys on tropical islands at your age if someone could actually stand you enough to stick around."

"Your powers of deduction never cease to amaze me."

"Give me your bed."

"No."

Andrew glared at him, hating that the big oaf couldn't even see it.

He touched the wet spot on his "bed" and pulled a face. There was no way he was lying on that. Andrew considered just flipping it over, but he knew the bottom was filthy and there were probably all kinds of bugs. Gross.

Logan, the asshole, started snoring softly.

Andrew smiled.

And then he plopped down on top of him.

The pained sound Logan made was goddamn music to his ears.

"The hell are you doing?" Logan growled.

Andrew settled more comfortably on top of him. "You should have just given me your bed," he said in his nicest tone. "I have nowhere to sleep, so I'm sleeping on you."

"Get off me." Logan tried to shove him off, but Andrew clung on stubbornly, his fingers digging into Logan's sides. Logan might have been bigger and stronger, but Andrew had more leverage in this position. And fuck, it was a matter of pride now. If he wasn't going to get sleep, neither would the asshole.

They wrestled, grunting, Logan swearing filthily under him. "Get off me, you monkey—"

Andrew broke into giggles as he held on, which quickly turned into hysterical laughter. It wasn't all that funny, to be honest, but his emotions were all over the place, and he had no idea what to do with them. He was freaking out of his mind; he had no idea what he was doing or what was happening to his life, he hated this man, couldn't stand him, but he also needed him with a ferocity that terrified him. He didn't know what was going on anymore—who he was, what he was, why this was happening—

"Have you lost your mind?" Logan growled. "Stop that—stop laughing!"

He didn't stop. Couldn't. He laughed, and laughed, until the noises leaving his throat became ugly and broken, his body shuddering and his eyes burning with tears.

Logan went rigid under him. "For fuck's sake," he said tersely. "If you start crying on me, I'll kick you outside."

Andrew tightened his grip on his sides. "I'm not crying," he said, his voice thicker than he would have liked.

Logan heaved a long-suffering sigh. He seemed irritated, but he wasn't attempting to shove him off anymore.

"Quit crying and sleep," he said at last.

Something inside Andrew loosened a little. He closed his eyes and breathed out.

The rain kept beating against the shelter's roof, but all Andrew could hear was the steady, strong beating of the heart under his ear.

He didn't even notice falling asleep.

Chapter 8

Logan had never been a particularly religious person. But he thought if God existed, the rain would stop by the morning and he'd able to escape the shelter.

If God existed, he clearly didn't give a damn about him. He woke up the next morning to the monotonous drumming of the rain.

Logan sighed and looked at the guy sprawled on his chest. The gaps in the shelter let in just enough daylight to see.

He stared at Andrew's deceptively sweet face, at his parted lips that kept brushing against Logan's chest every time he breathed, his long, dark eyelashes, and that smooth, golden skin.

Logan looked away and shoved the guy off him.

The confused cursing would have been amusing if Logan wasn't in such a shitty mood.

This had been a terrible idea. What had he been thinking?

"Dick," Andrew grumbled sleepily.

Logan got to his feet and went outside naked. He pissed, brushed his teeth, and then washed himself in the lukewarm rain, glowering at the gray sky.

He was tempted to just stay outside, the rain be damned, but no matter how warm it was, staying wet all day was a bad idea.

They couldn't afford getting sick. They didn't have any medicine. They were also running low on toothpaste and salt, and their blankets were becoming unsalvageable even without getting jizz all over them.

Logan ran a hand over his face, his shoulders sagging.

All right. What was done was done. There was no use crying over spilled milk. Last night had been a mistake, but he wouldn't repeat it. He'd just been frustrated. On edge. As long as he kept his dick out of that repressed little shit, it would be all right. One ill-advised sort-of-fuck didn't have to change anything.

Feeling a little better, Logan returned to the shelter.

Andrew was stretched out on his belly, sleeping peacefully on Logan's bedding. He was still naked.

Logan's jaw clenched, his newfound calm evaporating in a flash. He tore his eyes away from that bubble butt and kicked Andrew on the shin. "Get off my bed."

Andrew just mumbled something sleepily and ignored him.

Logan's eyes returned to that smooth, plump ass. He was only a man.

Tearing his gaze away again, Logan leaned down and growled into Andrew's ear, "Get. Off. My. Bed. Or I'll take it as an invitation to fuck you."

Andrew stiffened before sitting up so fast their heads nearly knocked.

He glared at Logan sleepily, raking a hand through his hair. "Fuck off," he said, his cheeks pink. "It's bad enough that you molested me last night. If you think I'll let you do—do…" His blush deepened, and he scowled, unable to meet Logan's eyes.

Snorting, Logan stretched out on his bedding. He watched through half-lidded eyes as Andrew just sat there, looking embarrassed and lost. Logan almost felt sorry for him—the guy clearly was freaking out about what had happened last night—except he didn't like Andrew enough to feel true sympathy for him. Mostly Andrew just annoyed him—and turned him on, which only annoyed him more. But fuck, he was lovely. His hair had grown out of his short haircut and now was a mess of light brown curls, and his plump lips were practically asking to be kissed or have a hard cock stretching them. And those ridiculous eyelashes—

"You done ogling me?" Andrew said.

"No," Logan said, letting his gaze travel down Andrew's body, his arousal spiking at seeing all that smooth, golden skin. His gaze lingered on Andrew's nipples, brown and pretty. He'd never thought nipples could be pretty, but somehow, Andrew's were.

Logan shifted his gaze to the ceiling, annoyed both with Andrew and himself.

Enough. He wasn't a goddamn teenager. He could keep it in his pants.

***

It set the pattern for the rest of the day.

Andrew kept sulking and making snide remarks about being molested the previous night—and how Logan was never allowed to put his dirty paws on him again—but he stuck close to Logan all the same.

Granted, their proximity was enforced by the rain, but Andrew really didn't have to sit quite as close to him while they ate their meager meal.

It put Logan in a shitty mood, his nerves raw and his body on edge.

As night fell, they stretched out on their pathetic "beds."

Logan stared at the ceiling of the shelter, listening to the rhythm of the falling rain. The sound was depressing. Lonely. It made him long for another person's warmth. For another person's touch—for *something*. He felt like crawling out of his own skin and doing something. Something ill-advised.

He knew Andrew wasn't asleep.

There was tension in the air, so thick he could almost taste it.

Finally, he couldn't stand it anymore.

He rolled onto his side and pressed his chest against Andrew's back.

Andrew let out a sigh that seemed both relieved and annoyed. "Fuck off."

Logan wrapped an arm around Andrew's waist and pressed them flush against each other, his erection nestling between Andrew's cheeks. "Stop making it complicated," he said, nipping at Andrew's nape. "It doesn't have to mean anything."

"But—"

"Shut up and jerk off. You know you want to."

After a long moment, he heard the telltale sound of flesh moving against flesh.

Burying his face against Andrew's nape, Logan closed his eyes and sought his own release.

It really meant nothing. Just two touch-starved, lonely humans seeking relief and comfort.

Nothing more.

But fuck, touching Andrew was oddly addictive.

Logan hadn't realized how much he'd missed having a warm, naked body in his arms. An orgasm was kind of secondary to the pleasure derived from physical contact.

He had intended to just grind against Andrew's ass while the other guy jerked off, but he felt greedy now. He wanted more. His hands started wandering, stroking Andrew's chest and stomach, kneading his pecs and brushing his nipples.

"Stop that," Andrew murmured weakly, but he didn't attempt to pull away and didn't stop stroking his own cock.

Logan ignored him, his face buried in Andrew's nape as his hand rubbed and tweaked those pretty nipples. Fuck, he wished he could suck on them.

He pinched the left nipple and Andrew whined, shuddering against him. Logan slid his hand lower, over Andrew's trembling stomach, and then lower, until his hand bumped against Andrew's.

The guy tensed up.

After a long beat, Andrew's hand dropped.

Logan wrapped his hand around the stiff cock.

Andrew let out a shaky breath. "I'm not gay," he said, haltingly.

Logan just scoffed. Andrew's cock was a nice size, a little shorter and slimmer than his own, and it was already leaking pre-come as Logan started stroking it.

"I'm not gay," Andrew said again, but his words came out more like a moan.

"I'm not hearing a no," Logan said, jacking him off.

"As if a no would stop you."

"You won't find out unless you try it," Logan said dryly, but he didn't press. He knew Andrew felt better about this if he could pretend that he was being forced.

Logan should have probably been more bothered by that, but he wasn't. Had he cared for Andrew or—God forbid—actually wanted a relationship with him, this would have been offensive as fuck. But as things stood, Andrew continuing being a bigoted little shit practically guaranteed that Logan wouldn't get attached. This meant nothing. Just a base need that didn't mean anything.

So he stroked Andrew's cock, deriving a sick sort of pleasure from every moan that bigoted straight guy let out as a "homo" jacked him off.

Andrew clearly was trying to be quiet, trying to swallow his noises, but soon enough, he couldn't stop his moans from slipping out of his mouth. His hips started moving too, fucking into Logan's fist helplessly until Andrew was a moaning, trembling mess.

"No—" Andrew cried out as Logan took his hand away.

"Turn around."

Andrew did as he was told, gasping.

"Touch my cock," Logan said.

"I won't."

Chuckling, Logan took Andrew's hand and wrapped it around his aching cock. "Jack it off."

"I'm not gay."

"Jack it off. Or I won't touch yours."

"I hate you," Andrew said, but his hand finally moved, a little hesitant at first. "This is disgusting."

"Shut up, or I'll shut you up with my cock."

That shut Andrew up.

"But maybe you'll like it," Logan said, pressing their foreheads together. He resumed stroking Andrew's cock. "Maybe that's what you actually want: a fat cock in your mouth—"

"Fuck off," Andrew said breathlessly, squeezing Logan's cock tighter and fucking into Logan's fist. "I'm not a—"

"Faggot? You have a cock in your hand, straight guy." Logan sucked on his jawline. "And you *like* it."

"No—" The word turned into a long moan as Andrew came into Logan's hand. "Oh."

Logan pushed Andrew's boneless body onto his back.

"My turn," he said, stroking his own cock with Andrew's come, getting it nice and slick.

The guy under him seemed barely conscious and allowed Logan to arrange his limbs the way he wanted them. Fuck, something about it went straight to Logan's cock. Having this confrontational, opinionated asshole so pliant and satisfied in his arms was beyond arousing. Logan put his slick cock between Andrew's thighs, squeezed them together, and then fucked them, hard and fast, until he saw stars.

He collapsed on top of Andrew, burying his face in his neck. He breathed, his body still shuddering with the afterglow.

He felt better than he had in months.

Chapter 9

The rain finally stopped on their eleventh day in the shelter.

It was too little, too late, but Andrew still felt relieved.

The enforced closeness had fucked everything up, not allowing him to put some much-needed distance between them—not allowing him to escape. A week. He'd had to put up with Logan groping and molesting him every night for a week, and Andrew's stupid, traitorous body had betrayed him every time—to Logan's amusement.

God, Andrew *hated* him.

He was so glad the rain had ended. They wouldn't have to live on top of each other anymore. The madness was finally over.

But as Andrew stretched out on his blanket under the clear starry sky, his heart was pounding and his skin was prickling with anxiety. He felt naked, even though he was wearing a t-shirt for once. He *couldn't* make himself relax, tensing up at every sound. He couldn't relax enough to sleep.

Squeezing his eyes shut, he focused on the sound of the ocean beating gently against the shore. It should have been calming. Soothing. But all it did was remind him of how small and insignificant he was compared to Mother Nature, how far from civilization they were.

He hugged himself, feeling illogically cold. He wondered if they held a funeral for him already. Probably.

He wondered who'd even come to his funeral.

He had to swallow the sudden lump in his throat. It didn't matter. Why did he care if people didn't come to his *funeral*? Had he been truly dead, he wouldn't have cared. Dead people didn't care about anything. Vivian was likely mourned by hundreds of people—everyone loved her—but it was a small comfort when she was dead. No one likely gave a fuck if Andrew was dead or alive, but so what? He didn't want people to mourn him. He didn't need people, period. He'd only ever needed Vivian, and now she was gone. His wife, his best friend, and his beloved. What did it matter if people he didn't give a fuck about didn't give a fuck about his death?

But no matter what he told himself, the cold, lonely feeling in the pit of his stomach didn't go anywhere. He felt achingly alone, and for the first time in years, he hated the feeling, couldn't stand it, felt like he was choking on it. It had been easy to be a loner when he still had a loving, supportive wife. Now he felt... He felt anchorless. Adrift. And any other word that meant *miserable*.

He wanted arms around him. He wanted not to be alone.

He wanted to feel wanted.

Andrew opened his eyes.

Then, he got to his feet and walked toward the other man's bedroll, his bare feet silent on the sand.

He looked down at Logan. The moonlight was bright enough to see that Logan's eyes were open. He was gazing up at Andrew, his expression impossible to read.

Andrew wet his dry lips, his heart pounding against his ribcage.

He pulled his t-shirt off. Then he hooked his thumbs on the waistband of his shorts and dragged them down. He stepped out of them, his eyes still locked with Logan's.

For a long moment, there was only silence as they stared at each other.

Then Logan pushed his own boxers down and pulled out his half-hard cock. It seemed huge in the moonlight. Obscene. "Get on your knees."

Andrew's knees suddenly felt weak.

He dropped to one knee, then the other, until he was settled between Logan's thighs.

Logan's hand buried in Andrew's overgrown hair and pulled him down. "Suck me off," he said, his voice low and hoarse.

Andrew closed his eyes and shook his head. "I'm not sucking your dick. I'm not gay."

Logan made a frustrated sound. "Then what the hell are you—"

"I'm not sucking your cock. Force me."

Logan's hand went very still.

Andrew was glad Logan couldn't see that he was blushing.

After a long, tense moment, Logan said, "All right. But you'll need a safeword."

Andrew frowned, bewildered. "What for?"

"I'm not forcing myself on you without a safeword, you twisted little fuck," Logan gritted out. "I need to know when you really mean it if you want me to stop."

Andrew scoffed. "You didn't ask for a safeword in the shelter."

"And it was wrong of me." Logan sighed. "I mean, I know you well enough by now, and I wouldn't have actually been that pushy if I wasn't sure you wanted it, but

I could still have misjudged the situation. Non-consent play can be dangerous, you little idiot."

"Don't call me an idiot. And I didn't want it!"

"Besides, this is different from handjobs," the asshole said, as if Andrew hadn't said anything. "Pick a safeword. Any word."

"Fine," Andrew grumbled unhappily. It wasn't what he'd wanted. Choosing a safeword would mean he was choosing this—and wasn't actually being forced. He didn't like it. But fine. "Funeral."

"Funeral? Your mind is a strange place."

Andrew didn't say anything. He looked down.

At Logan's cock. It was still hard.

Andrew licked his trembling lips. God, was he really going to allow another man to fuck his mouth? Had he lost his mind? What was he doing? He should leave. He should stop this. All he had to do was say the word.

But he remained silent, staring at the cock in morbid fascination. He'd touched it in the shelter, but he didn't really have the opportunity to look at it. It was so thick. And long. And hard. He'd made Logan hard. It was weirdly thrilling. Despite Logan's grumpy attitude, he *wanted* him. A body didn't lie.

His hand in Andrew's hair tightening, Logan yanked him down. "Suck."

The massive cock pushed into his mouth without any preamble. Andrew choked, his eyes widening.

Logan didn't give him time to adjust.

He just used him.

He fucked Andrew's mouth with no consideration for his comfort, hard and fast, as if Andrew's mouth was just a hole for his cock. It was incredibly degrading, but somehow it was exactly what he needed. It felt good.

He didn't have to think. He was nothing but a wet hole for Logan's cock.

Warmth spread through Andrew's body, his blood rushing to his cock. He whimpered around the thick cock in his mouth, choking on it and unable to get enough of this feeling. Logan was grunting above him, thrusting into his mouth as if possessed. "Yes, fuck, take it." His grip on Andrew's hair tightening, he held him down, his hips thrusting, and thrusting, and *thrusting*.

Andrew gagged a little as the cock repeatedly bumped against the back of his throat. It must have felt very good for Logan: he groaned and kept doing it, fucking his throat, no finesse or restraint, just pure animal need. Andrew couldn't think—it was probably lack of oxygen, but his mind felt hazy and slow. He liked it. It felt good. Like the strangest sort of high. He was wanted. He was wanted so much it made Logan lose control.

He let out a disappointed sigh as Logan's jizz hit the back of his throat.

Blinking dazedly, Andrew spat out what he couldn't swallow and dropped his head onto Logan's stomach. Oh, he felt wonderful. His cock was soft and sensitive in a way that indicated that he must have come, too. He didn't remember it, but he didn't care. He felt good. So good. Content.

Logan's voice snapped him out of it. "We should probably talk about this."

Andrew scrunched up his nose. "No, we really don't. There's nothing to talk about." Huh. His voice sounded wrecked.

"If you say so."

"I do say so. Now shut up. You're ruining the mood."

"I wasn't aware there was a mood."

"There was. It was called blessed silence."

Logan snorted. "Fine. But we really need to talk about it."

Andrew ignored him, his eyelids growing heavier by the minute.

It was odd, but now the sound of the ocean beating against the shore didn't make him feel lonely or small. It seemed like a calming lullaby.

Andrew let it lull him into sleep.

Chapter 10

Sometimes Logan wondered what the hell they were doing.

It didn't happen all that often. He generally dealt with the issue by not thinking about it. Not thinking about it was surprisingly easy when he had a hot guy sucking his dick whenever he wanted. Or rather, a hot guy letting him use his mouth whenever he wanted. The distinction was very clear—and one Andrew didn't let him forget about.

They really needed to talk about it. People generally didn't do that kind of thing without explicitly discussing what each party got from that kind of relationship. Not that it was a *relationship*. It was… a mutually beneficial arrangement, nothing more.

Logan knew it wasn't really about sex for Andrew. It wasn't about sex for him, either. Sex was just a way for them to feel less lonely. A physical affirmation of life and an escape route from it at the same time. A way to feel good, a release of tension. The sex was an escape, like drugs and alcohol. Orgasms were secondary almost to the point of unimportance. Sexual gratification didn't seem to be the main reason why Andrew liked sucking his cock—and he clearly liked it, no matter how much he liked to pretend that he was being forced.

At first Logan had been a little uneasy about the whole thing, but it was undeniable that the other man enjoyed having his mouth fucked.

"Enjoyed" might actually be an understatement. Logan had never met a guy who got off on having his mouth used as much as Andrew did: he could come from it completely untouched. Andrew also liked making him hard. He would sometimes reach out and touch Logan's cock for no reason and watch him get hard with a fascinated look in his eyes. Logan wasn't sure why Andrew liked it so much—Andrew's mind was a weird place and worked in mysterious ways. Logan didn't try to understand him. He didn't *want* to understand him. There was only one step from understanding someone to getting attached to them, and Logan wasn't doing it. Not with a guy who was a bigoted, repressed mess.

But fuck, Andrew looked so *soft* after he let Logan use his mouth: all flushed, glassy-eyed, and mellow. It did things to him. Things Logan had to nip in the bud. So he tried not to look at Andrew in those moments—if he did, he wanted to shove the guy under him and kiss him until he forgot his own name.

They didn't do kisses. Ever.

Anyway, everything was fine—as long as Logan didn't let himself think about things for more than a few seconds.

The situation was… manageable enough until one day, weeks after they'd started fooling around, everything went downhill.

Logan was looking at the horizon, watching the spectacular sunset, his cock half-hard in the other guy's mouth. He'd already come less than an hour ago, so the urgency wasn't there. He just liked keeping his cock in Andrew's mouth, to use him as a cock-warmer until he started hardening again. It was a kink he hadn't even known he had—until Andrew.

It also had the benefit of Andrew being quiet and mellow.

Absentmindedly, Logan scratched behind Andrew's ear.

A low sound, something like a purr, made him freeze.

He looked down at the guy seated on the sand between his legs. Andrew's eyes were closed, his pretty lips stretched wide by Logan's cock, an expression of utter contentment and peace on his face.

After a moment, Logan's hand moved again. Andrew purred like a pleased cat, leaning into his touch, his lips tightening around Logan's cock—which was now rock hard again.

Fuck.

Logan wrenched his eyes away and started thrusting into that mouth, hard and almost cruel.

It did nothing to erase the image of Andrew's content, lovely face from his mind.

***

It should have stopped at that. One weird display of inappropriate affection could have been easily written off.

But now Logan found himself unable to stop touching him after and during the blowjobs. Andrew reacted to a gentle touch *beautifully*: all but purring and leaning into the touch like a touch-starved kitten.

Logan had trouble believing it was Andrew's normal. It was probably just the isolation getting to him.

It was getting to Logan, too.

The more time passed, the blurrier his self-imposed rules became.

What did it matter that Andrew was a bigoted asshole when they were going to be stuck on this island for the rest of their lives? Neither of them was their real self here. The island had changed them both into something else. The real-world Logan normally avoided homophobic, latent homosexuals like the plague. The real-world Andrew would never suck a "homo's" cock.

Neither of those men existed on the island.

There was only here and now, the slick mouth around his cock and Andrew's glazed, drunk eyes as he gazed up at Logan as if he were a *god*.

Fucking hell.

Logan had never liked being needed.

Now he wanted it, craved it like his own personal drug.

***

Time passed strangely on the island.

It felt like the days crawled, and yet at the same time, they blurred together, and months flew by.

Logan wasn't sure when they'd started sleeping together. At some point he just realized that it'd been ages since Andrew had slept on his own bedding. The guy dozed with his head on Logan's stomach most of the time—when he didn't fall asleep with Logan's cock in his mouth.

The realization didn't freak Logan out as much as it probably should have.

He just shrugged mentally and figured it was only practical. Convenient. If Andrew slept with his head burrowed against Logan's stomach or thigh, it would be easier to slip his cock back into Andrew's mouth in the morning.

Sometimes Andrew sucked Logan's cock while Logan slept. Just on the tip of it, as if it were a giant pacifier. He really seemed more content with Logan's cock in his mouth, as if sucking Logan's cock *comforted* him. Logan probably shouldn't have found it as arousing as he did, but it was just another thing he'd stopped giving a fuck about. This whole arrangement was weird and surreal.

What was one more weird thing to add to the pile?

***

Andrew had six moles on his left arm and just two on his right arm. Logan traced them idly with his fingers when he had nothing better to do—and he rarely had something better to do.

Andrew allowed it. He seemed so used to his touch by now that he never reacted negatively when Logan touched him—just leaned into the touch like a flower turning toward the sun. It did terrible fucking things to Logan's insides.

He found himself touching Andrew more often with every day, until it became just something they did, all the time. They were rarely apart from each other for more than a few minutes. They did everything together, the concept of personal space long gone.

The one time Logan left their bedroll in the middle of the night to answer the call of nature, he had to run back to their camp when Andrew started calling out his name in a tight, panicked voice.

"Shhh, I'm here," Logan said, wrapping his arms around Andrew's shaking form.

Andrew clung to him, breathing raggedly, his face buried in Logan's neck.

"Just a nightmare," he said at last, clearly trying to save face.

They both knew it was a lie, but Logan didn't call him on it.

He understood.

He understood all too well.

***

That nightmare may not have been real, but Andrew had real nightmares too.

They never really talked about it, but Logan often woke up to Andrew burying his face against Logan's armpit and breathing oddly. Taking deep breaths. As if the scent of Logan's *sweat* calmed him. Grounded him in reality.

It was heartbreaking and terrifying. Terrifying and exhilarating.

Logan could no longer deny that he loved being needed by Andrew. He liked being relied on. He liked it a little too much to be healthy. The subconscious trust in Andrew's body language and attitude gave him such a rush, a thrill unlike any other.

He was addicted, in the worst possible way.

***

They had been on the island for seven months when Andrew got sick.

He was weak as a kitten, barely conscious, and his fever was so high his skin felt like a furnace to the touch.

Logan had no idea what was wrong: it wasn't like he was qualified in any way to diagnose him.

He could only observe him helplessly, feeling useless and angry, his chest tight with panic every time Andrew became unresponsive. He washed Andrew's body with a cool rag and hoped he was actually helping instead of making it worse.

It was the longest week of his life.

By the time Andrew's fever finally broke, Logan was mentally and physically wrung out, the tight ball of anxiety in his stomach refusing to dissipate completely.

Realistically, he had always known they were unlikely to live a long life on this island. Living in such poor conditions and eating barely edible, badly cooked meals was hardly conducive to a long life. He had always known that if they got sick, they wouldn't have any medical care or medicine. But this week had driven the point home in a way he hadn't realized before.

"I hope I'll die first," Andrew murmured that night, pressing his face into Logan's armpit.

Logan tightened his arms around him. "Shut up," he said hoarsely.

Truth be told, he selfishly hoped for the opposite.

Chapter 11

They had been on the island for eight months when Logan realized that they barely talked anymore. It wasn't that they didn't communicate; they did. They just didn't need words for that.

Their bodies were so attuned to one another at this point that words didn't seem necessary. Why use words when Logan could just lay his hand on Andrew's shoulder and turn him toward where he wanted him to look? Why use words when Andrew could just look at him in that particular way before dropping to his knees and swallowing down his cock? Words seemed redundant. There was nothing worth discussing going on in their life. Just them. And since they'd stopped arguing all the time and they both avoided talking about the *thing* between them, they didn't really have anything to talk about. Even Andrew's talking-at-night phase had ended a while ago. Now he seemed to prefer dozing quietly with his head on Logan's stomach while Logan's fingers played with his hair.

It wasn't normal. But then again, nothing about this situation was fucking normal.

Or rather, their normal wasn't what anyone else would consider normal.

They did have something of a routine.

They woke up, he fucked Andrew's mouth, they ate whatever they could fish or forage, or their tomatoes. (It sometimes messed him up when he thought about the fact that they had been stranded on this island long enough to harvest their second crop of tomatoes.)

After eating, they ran several laps around the island to keep themselves in shape, and then dozed for a while under the canopy of palms, with Andrew on top of him, his face buried in Logan's happy trail or against his chest. Normal people would probably call it cuddling. Logan didn't call it anything, but it was his favorite part of the day. Peaceful. Companionable. The closest to happy he'd been since the plane crash.

He was usually awakened by a wet mouth around his cock. After sleepily fucking Andrew's mouth, he watched Andrew get himself off, running his fingers through Andrew's hair and stroking his neck and back. Sometimes he sucked Andrew's cock if Andrew didn't feel too weird about it that day.

Sometimes they didn't even touch each other sexually—just touched for the sake of it, and that was enough. Then they ate—and then the circle repeated itself.

The routine was almost comforting despite having a surreal quality to it.

It wasn't a relationship.

It wasn't even sex for the sake of it. It was a need. A necessity.

But it was simple. It was familiar.

It was all they had.

***

Their routine was broken by a huge storm.

They didn't bother with the shelter—it wouldn't withstand this kind of storm, so they huddled under a palm tree, Logan's arms locked around Andrew from behind. Just for balance, of course.

His chin on Andrew's shoulder, Logan looked at the raging ocean, wondering when the storm would finally stop.

Something white on the horizon caught his gaze.

For a moment, Logan's brain didn't seem to comprehend what he was seeing.

But the longer he watched, the more certain he became. His eyes weren't playing tricks on him. There really was a ship—some kind of yacht—heading toward the island. Though "heading" didn't seem to be an accurate description: the speed with which it was approaching the island was rather unsafe. The ship had been likely knocked off its course because of the storm. In the nine months they had been on the island, they hadn't seen a single ship.

But now…

Andrew made a questioning sound, and Logan realized that he might have squeezed him too hard in his excitement.

Excitement. Was that what he was feeling? Logan didn't know. But his heart was pounding, his body tense and alert for what felt like the first time in forever. It felt almost as though he was waking up from some bizarre dream.

"What?" Andrew said, his voice hoarse from lack of use.

"The ship," Logan said, his voice equally hoarse.

Andrew went rigid before straightening up from his slouch against Logan's chest.

Logan couldn't see his face from his position behind him, but he could see Andrew's muscles stiffen as he saw the ship, too.

"It's heading our way," Logan said, rather unnecessarily.

Andrew didn't say anything for a moment.

Then, he all but scrambled away from Logan and got to his feet. He ran toward the shore.

Logan followed him after a moment, feeling oddly numb.

They were going to be rescued.

Rescued.

The thought was… strange.

Obviously he was happy. Beyond happy. But it was still strange. It didn't seem real.

But it was.

The yacht dropped anchor in the island's tiny bay, its crew clearly intending to wait out the bad weather there.

They swam toward the yacht, not even bothering to grab their things—they could always come back for them later. The raging ocean was nearly impossible to navigate. Logan grabbed Andrew's arm when he disappeared under the high waves and squeezed it. *Keep close.*

Andrew nodded.

It seemed to take forever before they reached the yacht.

The moment Logan heard surprised shouts as the people on the yacht noticed them, a surreal feeling hit him again. Those people were speaking English. Hearing a voice that wasn't his or Andrew's after nine months was something of a shock.

Numb and disoriented, he climbed behind Andrew onto the deck and allowed other people to pull him up. Hands touching his shoulders. Hands that weren't Andrew's. It was fucking weird.

"Who are you?" someone said, wrapping a blanket around him. "What the hell are you doing here?"

Logan didn't reply. Couldn't.

His eyes met Andrew's. He was staring at Logan with wide eyes, looking equally lost and dazed, the way he looked when he wanted to be held.

Logan's fingers twitched toward him. He balled them into fists.

They had been rescued.

It was over.

Everything was over.

PART II

Chapter 12

Boston greeted them with sunshine.

Andrew slowly descended the steps of the private jet that Logan's family had sent for them—well, for Logan. He watched as two young women, likely Logan's sisters, hugged Logan tightly, their eyes wet and their smiles radiant. A warm family reunion. It must have been nice.

Andrew turned away from the emotional scene and just stood there for a moment, unsure what to do.

The past three days since they'd been rescued had been kind of crazy: medical checkups, interviews, endless phone calls, and then the long flight back to the US. The latter had made him so anxious Andrew had to be medicated for the rest of the flight. He still felt off balance. The sheer noise of the airport was overwhelming, and he had to breathe deeply to stop a panic attack. It was fine. He was back home. He would get used to the noise again.

A cab. He needed to get a cab. A cab would take him to Rutledge Manor. The Rutledges were likely waiting for him. Probably. Maybe. Andrew had called them and told them that he was alive and when he was going to arrive. The conversation had been… awkward, to say the least. Andrew wasn't even offended that Derek Rutledge's only question had been about Vivian.

Telling his brother-in-law that his only sister really was dead would forever be among the most uncomfortable conversations of his life.

And now he was back. Back home.

Home. Was Rutledge Manor still his home? He'd lived there for nine years with his wife, but now that Vivian was gone, he doubted he would be welcome to stay. He still needed to go there. All of his things were there—if the Rutledges hadn't gotten rid of them.

He needed to go. Find a cab. Go to the Rutledges.

Go.

Andrew's feet didn't move. They didn't listen to the commands of his brain at all.

He couldn't fucking move. Helplessly, he looked back at Logan. He found Logan already looking at him over the shoulder of the woman hugging him.

Their gazes locked.

Andrew wasn't sure what emotion was on his face, but Logan said something to his sisters and headed toward him.

Andrew watched him approach, still thrown off balance by how different Logan looked in clothes. This clean-shaven man in a sharp business suit looked nothing like the unshaven, half-naked guy Andrew had become… used to. It was disorienting.

"Going home?" Logan said, stopping a few feet away from him.

Andrew nodded, pursing his lips tightly.

Logan shoved his hands into the pockets of his jacket, his dark eyes unreadable. "See you around, then," he said after a moment.

Andrew opened his mouth and then closed it without saying anything. There was nothing to say. He nodded.

They stared at each other some more.

Behind Logan, someone cleared their throat. "You must be Andrew! I'm Alice, Logan's sister."

Andrew tried not to flinch. He forced a smile and said something to the young woman who hooked her arm with Logan's. She smiled and said something back. Andrew said something again. Small talk. They were making small talk. It was bizarre, after months of barely speaking. He thought he'd even managed to make some jokes, but he wasn't sure. Everything felt too much and somehow not real enough at the same time. It all felt like a dream, Logan's unreadable face the only thing in focus.

Somehow, Andrew ended up letting Alice and Kate—the other sister—talk him into dropping him off at the Rutledges' place. He climbed into the backseat of Kate's car and sat down next to Logan while Alice took the front passenger seat.

The sisters talked non-stop the entire ride about everything and nothing, catching Logan up with the lives of their relatives and mutual acquaintances. It flew right over Andrew's head.

He couldn't *focus*.

All he could think about was the warmth of Logan's body next to his and the inch that separated their knees.

It had been three days since they'd been this close. Not since the island.

Andrew clenched his jaw. Why was he even thinking about this? It was over. Whatever madness—whatever sickness—had possessed him on the island was gone now that they were back to their real lives. He was glad he could return to his normal life. A life without Logan. He was fucking ecstatic.

Logan tapped him on his knee with his fingers.

Andrew stiffened, his heart jumping into his throat. He turned his head to Logan. *What?* He was disgusted that he didn't even need to say that for Logan to understand him. It seemed the past few days hadn't been enough for them to lose the near-telepathy they'd developed on the island.

Logan cocked his head to the side slightly, his dark eyes questioning. *You okay?*

Pressing his lips together, Andrew gave a clipped nod. The place where Logan's fingers were touching him was burning. Or at least it felt like it.

Logan studied him for a moment, a wrinkle between his dark brows. "You just look like you're going to be sick."

"I'm not going to be sick," Andrew said unconvincingly, dropping his eyes. His gaze settled on the V of Logan's legs, on the outline of his cock, and his mouth suddenly filled with saliva. God, he'd give anything to have that cock in his mouth right now—the comforting hardness, girth, and warmth of it, moving in his mouth, using him, how good it felt to be just a vessel for it, a—

"Andrew," Logan ground out.

He snapped his gaze up—and encountered a pinched, annoyed expression on Logan's face.

Logan glared at him.

His face hot, Andrew glared back. What?

"Andrew?" Alice said. "We're almost there, I think."

Wrenching his gaze away from Logan, Andrew looked out the window and stared at the handsome mansion they were approaching.

The gates were open—so the Rutledges hadn't forgotten about his arrival, after all—and the car stopped in front of the house.

"Thanks," Andrew managed.

Kate smiled at him kindly. "You're very welcome! It's the least we could do to thank you for keeping our brother company on that godforsaken island."

Alice chuckled. "Consider it an apology," she said with a teasing smile at her brother. "He must have been insufferable."

Andrew smiled wanly. "Oh, absolutely," he said. "Thanks. See you."

He opened the door and all but stumbled out of the car. He took his bag out of the trunk and then stood there, rooted to the spot, as the car took off.

Something twisted his insides into a hard knot as the car disappeared out of sight. He took a deep breath, then another, trying to get rid of the tight feeling in his chest. He wasn't going to panic. He wasn't on the island anymore. He didn't need Logan. He was fine.

He was fine.

Andrew turned around and stared at the mansion. He'd expected to feel some kind of relief at seeing it. It had been his home for nine years. But all he felt was a sense of loss and dread. How could he enter it without Vivian? It felt like he had no right to do it.

He was being stupid. The Rutledges might not like him much, but they weren't senseless or cruel.

Andrew forced himself to move.

Every step made the ball of anxiety in his chest tighten and harden until he felt nearly sick with it. His heart beat hard against his ribcage, so fast that he felt nearly dizzy. Was he having a panic attack?

At last, after what felt like forever, he reached the front door.

It opened.

It was a butler.

Andrew didn't recognize him. He must have been new, but it seemed he had been warned about Andrew.

He followed the butler to the living room. Andrew wanted to tell him that he knew the way, but then he thought better of it. It wasn't like it was his home anymore.

As soon as he entered the room, Derek Rutledge's dark eyes met his.

Andrew swallowed, acutely aware of the empty space beside him where Vivian would have been. Should have been.

"Welcome back," Derek said curtly before turning and walking out of the room.

Shawn, Derek's husband, winced a little. "Don't take it personally," he said. "We're glad you're alive. Derek…Vivian's death hit him hard. When we got the news that a few people survived the crash after all and you were one of the survivors…" He shrugged, an uncomfortable look crossing his face. "Derek didn't really talk about it, but I think he got his hopes up that Vivian might be alive. And now he has to grieve her again, in a way."

Andrew gave a clipped nod. "It's fine. I understand."

A strained silence descended upon the room.

He and Shawn had never really gotten along. They'd gotten off to a bad start—Andrew hadn't managed to hold his tongue and had publicly insulted him—and it always seemed to taint their interactions, no matter how many years had passed since then. Andrew didn't know what to do about it. Vivian had always urged him to talk to Shawn and clear the air between them, but Andrew didn't want to.

He'd always been bad at talking about his mistakes, and it wasn't as though he'd been entirely wrong about Shawn—the guy had clearly been sleeping with Derek because of his money at the time.

It didn't matter that they were in love with each other now—Andrew *had* been right, dammit.

"Anyway," Shawn said, finally breaking the awkward silence. "You're probably tired after the flight. Take a nap if you want. We'll have dinner later."

Andrew looked away. "I'm not staying," he said. "I'll pack my things and will be out of your hair in a few hours."

Silence.

"Oh," Shawn said. "Okay, then."

Andrew pursed his lips, hating that a part of him wanted the Rutledges—someone, *anyone*—to say that they wanted him to stay. *Or stay for him.*

Stupid. Fucking pathetic.

He turned to head upstairs when a thought stopped him. "Who's been doing my job while I was presumed dead?" He hoped it wasn't his brother-in-law. Derek might be highly intelligent—he was a professor at Harvard—but he had no idea how to run a company like Rutledge Enterprises.

"Um," Shawn said, sounding even more uncomfortable. "We kind of had a revolving door of people who had the CEO position. In the end, we gave up and signed a partnership deal with the Caldwell Group. Ian Caldwell has been the CEO the last couple of months until—"

"Ian Caldwell," Andrew said before whirling around and staring at Shawn incredulously. "The man whose baby sister sliced her wrists when Derek humiliated her by publicly breaking off their engagement? That Ian Caldwell?"

Shawn winced, looking sheepish and pained. "To be fair to us, we had no idea he was her brother. They have different surnames."

Unbelievable.

Andrew pinched the bridge of his nose. "Does the company even exist anymore?" Ian Caldwell was a shark. A few months would be enough for him to do major damage to the company of the man he had every reason to dislike.

Shawn's grimace wasn't exactly encouraging. "It does. The problem is, he sneaked in some seemingly harmless clauses in the contract we signed, so now he basically has unlimited power over the company."

Great.

Just fantastic.

"And now it's gotten even more complicated," Shawn said, running a hand over his face. "Caldwell had an accident recently and is still in a coma. It doesn't look good for him."

Andrew frowned, struggling to keep up. He'd always had a sharp mind, but he was seriously out of practice after months of barely using it. The nine months of mind-numbing routine would do that to anyone.

"But the thing is," Shawn said, raking a hand through his blond hair. "All our agreements with the Caldwell Group still stand, and Caldwell's people are still in charge of the company now."

"Didn't you have a lawyer look over the contract before you signed it?" Andrew gritted out. That sounded like a fuck-up of gigantic proportions.

"We did," Shawn said, rather defensively. "But it looks like Caldwell bought his silence. You know Derek and I aren't used to all the business language, and reading through the fifty pages of that contract was like reading something in another language. We trusted the lawyer, and he let us down. That's all."

He sighed. "And you know Derek wanted nothing to do with his father's company. He didn't want to waste his time on it, so he was eager to get rid of the responsibility."

Andrew snorted. "Looks like he got that wish. Fine. I'll deal with it first thing in the morning."

"You don't have to," Shawn said, a look of discomfort flashing over his stupidly pretty face.

"I know," Andrew said. "But someone has to, and it isn't going to be you."

He strode away, feeling exasperated, irritated—and kind of relieved to have a purpose. Derek and Shawn may not have wanted him around, but they still needed him to get them out of the shit they'd landed their company in while Andrew was presumed dead. He was needed. He had a purpose again.

Part of him registered that it wasn't the most healthy way of thinking, but he discarded it. It was going to be all right. He just needed to relearn how to live his real life.

This… anxiety would go away soon.

It had to.

Chapter 13

It turned out that Shawn wasn't kidding when he said that Caldwell's people were now in charge of Rutledge Enterprises. Andrew spent the next few days alternating between reading the contract and—politely—arguing with Caldwell's people.

Reading the contract was an exercise in frustration: he was torn between admiring Ian Caldwell for managing to sneak so many loopholes into the contract and being frustrated at the Rutledges for falling for it. Had he been there, he would have never let—

But he hadn't been there.

No one let him forget that. Even though he didn't live at Rutledge Manor anymore, Vivian's ghost—and the island—seemed to follow him everywhere. The pitying looks were bad enough, but the curious ones were even worse. What was it like? Surviving a plane crash? Being stranded on a desert island for so long? Was it horrible? What did he do with his time?

The questions made him want to scream. He'd been trying so hard not to think about the island, but people kept reminding him of it over and over, their curiosity insatiable. What was it like? What was it like? What was it like?

It drove him crazy. It didn't help that he still struggled with being around people, their gazes, their attention, their *voices* making his skin crawl.

He kept waiting for the terrible disconnect to go away, wanting to feel normal again, but so far it hadn't happened. He didn't feel better. In fact, the knot in his chest seemed to become tighter with every passing day. He felt jittery and distracted, and half of the time he felt as if he didn't know what to do with himself—in the most literal and physical sense.

Enough. He needed to focus on work.

Andrew left his office—his new, temporary office—and headed to his old one. It was occupied by the vice president of the Caldwell Group, who was performing the functions of the CEO while Ian Caldwell was incapacitated.

He wasn't really looking forward to the conversation.

To be fair, the man was an experienced executive with a fantastic reputation in business circles, but Andrew wasn't really in the mood to be fair. First he'd lost the company he'd slaved over for years to Derek Rutledge; now he'd lost his position of CEO thanks to Derek's unwillingness to give a fuck about said company. Andrew had read the contract; he knew that had Derek bothered to read it, he would have seen the small print. But he clearly hadn't given a damn, and now Andrew had to clean up after his mess.

Fuck, he wanted a drink. He wanted—

He wanted Logan.

Andrew cringed and shoved the thought out of his mind. Or tried to. He knew it would be back. It always was. God, he hated these needy thoughts that sneaked back into his mind every twenty minutes.

He didn't fucking need Logan.

The sooner he forgot about everything that had happened on the island, the better. It hadn't been real. *This* life was real.

Sighing, he murmured a greeting to the CEO's assistant, a young, harried-looking blond guy. "Is he in?" he said, nodding toward the closed door.

The guy—Nate—pulled a face. "The demon? Is he ever not?"

Andrew made a sympathetic sound. He'd heard that Raffaele Ferrara was a nightmare to work for. The Italian was a major shareholder of the Caldwell Group and its vice president and COO. Only Ian Caldwell had more power in the company than Ferrara did. But while Ian Caldwell had the reputation of a demanding employer, Raffaele Ferrara had the reputation of a tyrant. His poor assistant looked like he hadn't slept in days.

"Please tell him I want to talk to him," Andrew said.

Nate nodded and pushed the button of the intercom. "Mr. Reyes wants to speak to you, Mr. Ferrara."

A deep voice replied dismissively, "I'm busy. I don't have time for him."

Andrew flushed. This was his company, dammit. Had been.

"Don't be a dick," Nate said.

Andrew blinked, staring at him in amazement.

"You're forgetting yourself," Ferrara said in a very soft voice.

Nate swallowed, but his voice didn't betray his nervousness as he said stubbornly, "But you're being one, *sir*. With all due respect. After what Mr. Reyes has been through, the least you can do is treat him—"

"Fine," Ferrara bit out. "Let him enter."

Nate switched the intercom off and gestured to Andrew to go into the office. "I wish I could say he isn't as much of a dick as he sounds, but he's actually worse," he said, sighing and then yawning.

"Go on. It's like pulling teeth."

"Unpleasantly difficult?"

"That too. But I meant that the more you drag it out, the worse it is. The word 'patience' isn't in his vocabulary."

Well, that wasn't exactly encouraging.

When Andrew entered the office, Ferrara looked up at him from his laptop and gave him a flat look. "Did you want something?"

His voice dripped with dismissiveness, and Andrew found his insides clenching.

He had always hated being dismissed. He hated that a part of him wanted to run out of this room like a little boy and hide.

He didn't, of course.

He forced himself to hold the man's gaze firmly. "Yes," he said. "My employees have been complaining to me about your methods."

Ferrara's eyes bored into him. They were unnerving, truth be told. Raffaele Ferrara was an objectively handsome man, his facial features and olive skin making his Mediterranean roots obvious, but something about his gaze was highly unsettling. The shape of his black eyebrows and his sharp, hawk-like black eyes made him look like a predator. His gaze was heavy, haughty, and condescending. Almost cruel.

"Your employees?" Ferrara said, his voice toneless. "Do you mean my employees?"

Andrew clenched his hand into a fist. The urge to leave was becoming irresistible. "No, my employees. I may not be the CEO anymore, but I own ten percent of the company."

Ferrara's thin lips curled into something that wasn't quite a smile.

"Derek Rutledge is the majority shareholder, and he has signed the contract that gave the Caldwell Group the right to run his company. If you have any objections, you're welcome to give them to Derek Rutledge." And he turned back to his computer, a clear dismissal.

Andrew opened his mouth and then closed it.

He'd never felt so helpless in his life. So useless. So small.

"I have been the CEO of this company for years," he finally managed. "It's very arrogant of you to reject my help."

Ferrara didn't even glance at him. "I don't need anyone's help," he said coldly. "And if people run to you to complain about me, tell them to come to me with their complaints—if they're so brave." He started typing, his gaze on his computer. "You're not needed, Reyes. Frankly, I'm surprised you've returned to work so soon after the ordeal. I doubt your mental health is where it needs to be."

Andrew pressed his lips together. "I'm fine," he said, shoving his hands into his pockets. They were shaking. "I'm ready to return to my job."

"I understand that you may think so," Ferrara said, his voice still flat. "But I'm afraid I can't give you back this office unless Ian tells me to do so."

"Caldwell is in a coma and is unlikely to ever wake up," Andrew bit out. "He isn't going to tell you jack shit."

Ferrara's black eyes shifted back to him. "Are you also a doctor now? He's breathing. He may wake up yet."

Andrew decided not to voice his doubts about it. He'd heard somewhere that Raffaele Ferrara and Ian Caldwell were pretty good friends—as much as two ruthless assholes could be friends.

"In any case, the point is moot," Ferrara said.

"You saw the documents we provided. The contract between Rutledge Enterprises and the Caldwell Group makes it clear that the Caldwell Group's CEO will be managing both companies for the duration of the partnership deal. And that person is me while Caldwell is unavailable. Am I speaking a language you don't understand?" His tone was final, dismissive, as if he were speaking to a stupid, annoying child.

Feeling angry, helpless, and utterly humiliated, Andrew turned and left the office.

His hands were shaking so badly by this point that he had to ball his fingers into fists.

He couldn't remember getting back, but he must have, because the next thing he was aware of, he was huddled on the couch in his office, his knees drawn up to his chest and his head between them as he tried to breathe through the waves of nausea.

He wasn't needed. He wasn't needed even here. No one needed him. No one wanted him around. The only person who had ever wanted—loved—him was dead, taking with her every good thing in his life. Now he was nothing. He was useless. He was wanted by no one.

I never wanted him. I'll never understand people who want children. All that boy did was ruin my cousin's life—and now my career too.

"Shut up," he whispered, pressing his hands to his ears, as if that would stop the voice in his head. It didn't. It never really did. Those words were one of his first memories, his aunt's annoyed tone as clear in his mind as if it had happened yesterday and not almost thirty years ago.

He'd always been proud of not letting his childhood define him. Sure, it hadn't been the best, but it hadn't been the worst, either. It had been fine.

He might not have grown up in a loving environment, but he'd had it better than most orphans. His childhood had been fine. He had been fed, clothed, and he'd had a roof over his head. No one abused him. It had been fine. He didn't need anyone to love him.

Except it seemed he still was the same pathetic, insecure little boy who had tried to pretend he didn't hear his aunt's words as she complained to her friends about being saddled with raising him after her cousin had died—*because no one else wanted him*—and how he ruined his mother's life when she'd gotten pregnant with him, not allowing her to pursue her dreams of college, and how Andrew was the sole reason his aunt couldn't accept a lucrative job offer she'd gotten.

Aunt Rebecca wasn't a bad woman. By all standards, she was a good one: self-sacrificing and generous. She had been just twenty-five when she had taken him in after his mother's death at the hand of a mugger. Although he called her "Aunt," she was his mother's cousin, not a close relative. She had raised him even though she didn't have to.

Andrew appreciated the sacrifices she had made for him, and he showed his appreciation to this day, supporting her financially and visiting her on holidays. He was grateful to her. He was.

But there was a reason he always felt emotionally drained after a visit to her. There was a reason he had always dragged Vivian with him when he visited Aunt Rebecca. Having his wife beside him, his kind, lovely, amazing wife who had chosen him, who had *wanted* him, was the only thing that made those visits bearable.

Not good enough, Andrew. You aren't trying hard enough. You can do better. Try harder.

His aunt's voice echoed in his head, the words she'd said all his life. Never quite pleased. Always a disapproving frown on her face. And him, the boy who owed her everything, trying and failing to please her again and again. Even his first job at Rutledge Enterprises was the result of his aunt's pushing. No matter what he did, it wasn't good enough. His marriage to Vivian was probably the only thing his aunt had ever approved of.

He hadn't gone to see his aunt after his return. He knew he should do it. Aunt Rebecca had wasted her best years on raising him, a child she'd never wanted. He owed her a visit. He dreaded it, now more than ever.

Fuck, it was so stupid. He was a grown man. He shouldn't have been scared of seeing one small, middle-aged woman, just because he had never been good enough for her.

But with Vivian gone, he had nothing to hide behind anymore. He was still as unwanted and unneeded as he was thirty years ago. A man who outlived his usefulness. A man who shouldn't have outlived his wife. It was *her* everyone wanted back, not him. Even Aunt Rebecca was fonder of Vivian than she had ever been of him. Andrew being back just reminded everyone that Vivian was dead while he was alive.

Maybe he should have died with her.

Maybe he should have stayed on the island and let everyone think he was dead.

He suddenly *yearned* for it, for the sheer simplicity of that life. It might have been weird, messed up, and downright unhealthy, but at least on the island he hadn't felt as though he was insufficient, unneeded, or wanting. He hadn't felt so useless.

He had felt… he had felt content.

"Are you fucking serious?" he whispered with a hoarse laugh.

He needed help if he seriously thought being stranded on the island was better than his normal life. Maybe he'd gone crazy after all. Maybe this was all a weird dream, and he would wake up any moment now to Logan's hand threading through his hair and the heavy, comforting weight of Logan's cock in his mouth.

Andrew flushed. Fuck, he really needed help. He shouldn't long for the *comforting* feeling of a cock in his mouth, what the hell. How messed up was that? He wasn't a… He wasn't gay. He was normal. What had happened on the island didn't matter. He didn't want to suck Logan's dick. He didn't miss sucking Logan's dick—or miss him, period. The island had just fucked him up. That was all.

This sickening longing… it would pass.

It had to.

Chapter 14

Vivian's funeral was on a Friday.

Andrew stood by the Rutledges and stared at the coffin numbly, trying to feel something other than unease and discomfort.

He hadn't been sure how he felt about Vivian's body being transferred from the island to be buried next to the other Rutledges, but he hadn't said no when Vivian's family asked for his opinion. Now he was beginning to regret it.

It was just strange. He felt like a fraud among all these crying people. He felt so guilty for no longer feeling grief. He was sad, of course, and he missed her, but that pain was duller now, tinged with affection and good memories. He'd had time to grieve his wife. He'd *buried* her with his own hands ten months ago. It didn't feel right to have her funeral again when he felt so far removed from that time.

He was glad for his dark sunglasses. He didn't need more judgmental looks than he already got.

Finally, after what felt like forever, it was over.

Andrew hurriedly walked away, the knot in his chest lessening with every step he took. God, why wasn't this getting easier? Why couldn't he stay among other people without feeling like he wanted to jump out of his own skin?

"Andrew!"

He cringed but stopped at the sound of his aunt's voice.

"Yes, Aunt Rebecca?" he said, turning around reluctantly.

His aunt was glaring at him. "You have been back for two weeks, but you haven't bothered to visit me even once. I had to find out about your survival from the news!"

"I'm sorry," he said. "I meant to visit you, but things have been crazy, you know—"

"No, I *don't* know," she said, her tone scathing. "Because you haven't even bothered to call me, you ungrateful, heartless boy."

Andrew tugged at his collar, but found the top button of his shirt already undone. He wasn't actually choking. It was all in his head. "I'm sorry. I'll do better, Auntie," he said, looking around desperately for an escape route. Any excuse to leave.

None was presenting itself. No one seemed interested in approaching him, everyone too busy offering their condolences to Vivian's grandmother and brother. Never mind that he was her husband.

Swallowing the bitter taste in his mouth, Andrew said, "I just got caught up in the legal issues, I swear. I'll visit you soon—"

"This Sunday," Aunt Rebecca said in a tone that brooked no argument.

"Right. On Sunday," Andrew said, forcing a smile onto his face.

Dammit.

***

After the funeral, Andrew went to a liquor store and bought a few bottles of cheap whiskey.

Vivian had liked expensive red wine, but Andrew's tastebuds didn't notice any difference between a bottle that cost a thousand dollars and one that cost ten. He used to buy high-end booze anyway, pretending that he knew the difference. Well, he had no one to pretend for anymore.

He returned to his hotel room and got smashingly drunk.

At least this time no one was there to judge him.

The memory of dark eyes looking at him disapprovingly flashed to the forefront of his mind, and he was hit with a wave of unbearable, crushing *longing*. Normally he pushed these thoughts—these feelings—away, tried to squash them down, but he was too drunk for that now.

He reached for his phone and opened Chrome with unsteady fingers.

In his defense, looking Logan up was laughably easy. Information about him was in every article about their miraculous survival.

Logan McCall. Thirty-four years old. An owner of a rather popular hotel chain.

Andrew's lips curled into a faint smile. He'd suspected that Logan wasn't a simple owner of a hotel when his family had sent a goddamn private jet for him, but this was kind of funny. Way to downplay one's business.

Apparently, Logan's family lived near Boston, but he lived by himself in NYC. His address and phone number obviously weren't listed anywhere, but it wouldn't be hard to find out. All he had to do was go to one of Logan's hotels and talk the manager into giving him Logan's number.

After all, everyone and their dog now knew that he had been Logan's fellow plane crash survivor. The manager was unlikely to refuse to give Logan's number to the person he had spent nine months living—surviving—with.

After looking up the nearest hotel that belonged to Logan, Andrew grabbed his unpacked suitcase, tossed in the few things he'd bothered to pull out of it, and called a cab.

As he stood in front of Logan's hotel, a sliver of doubt crept into his alcohol-addled mind. He shook it off and went inside.

"I'd like a room," he said at reception. He was pretty proud of himself for not slurring.

"Of course, sir. Your ID please," the woman said with a polite smile that didn't quite mask the curious look in her eyes. So she had recognized him. Considering how often his face had been plastered next to her boss's, it probably shouldn't have been surprising. Oh, well. Maybe it was for the best.

Giving her his ID, Andrew said quietly, "I have another request. I need Logan McCall's phone number."

The woman's eyes widened slightly. "I'll have to ask the manager," she said, her voice hesitant. "We don't give Mr. McCall's private information to anyone, but… I'll ask." She added softly, "And I'm sorry for your loss, Mr. Reyes."

The sincere sympathy in her voice made his chest hurt. "Thanks," Andrew said, clearing his throat a little. He didn't like that his private life had become so public, but it was what it was.

After being given the key card, he headed to his room, already wondering if he'd made a mistake. He had a feeling his sober self wasn't going to appreciate this tomorrow.

The room was nice and tastefully decorated, but Andrew kept fixating on the fact that it was Logan's hotel. It was probably fucked up and ridiculous, but the mere thought that all of this belonged to Logan made him feel oddly comfortable here. Yeah, it was beyond ridiculous.

He undressed and fell into the bed.

The mattress felt like a soft cloud. The sheets smelled clean and pleasant. He was tired. So, so tired. But sleep still refused to come to him. It was a problem he'd had for weeks, ever since… his return. He'd say he couldn't remember the last time he'd gotten a full night's sleep, but that would be a lie. He knew.

Andrew didn't know how long he'd lain like that, his face buried in the pillow and his mind drifting on the edge of sleep when the phone by the bed went off.

Reaching out, he answered it. "Hello?"

"Why are you in my hotel?"

Andrew's eyes flew open, his heart jumping into his throat.

It was stupid, but he hadn't actually thought about what he was going to say when he called Logan. He hadn't expected Logan to call *him*. Logan was calling him. Logan wanted to talk to him.

Andrew found himself smiling stupidly into his pillow. Hey, he was drunk. Drunk people could smile for no reason, right?

"Why do people go to a hotel?" he mumbled evasively. "I needed a place to stay at."

"Are you drunk?"

Andrew wasn't sure what it said about him that he'd missed that judgmental tone.

He was being stupid. But then again, drunk people were stupid.

"So what if I am?" he slurred, unsure why he wasn't bothering to hide his inebriated state anymore. He could if he made an effort, as he'd done when he'd spoken to the receptionist. But it was *Logan*. His body seemed to think it was perfectly fine to act like a whiny, stubborn child now. It was Logan. Logan. Logan had seen him at his worst.

"At least you aren't denying it," Logan said dryly.

Andrew said nothing. He wasn't even sure anymore what they were talking about, his eyelids becoming heavier as he listened to Logan's breathing. This felt… so familiar. Disturbingly comforting in its familiarity. All that was missing was a hard body pressed against his back or better yet, a… He pushed his thumb into his mouth and made a contented noise as he sucked on it.

"Christ, are you jerking off?"

Andrew froze. "No," he said around his thumb.

"You're lying."

"Am not."

"You're doing *something*. I know how you sound when you—" Logan cut himself off, muttering something frustrated under his breath. "Tell me."

The demanding edge to his voice made a shiver run through Andrew's body. He pulled his thumb out of his mouth and blinked at it as the realization of what exactly he was longing for hit him.

He flushed.

What was wrong with him, seriously?

"This is all your fault," Andrew complained. "You got me used to— things, and now I feel all messed up and on edge without…"

Without your cock in my mouth. Without your smell all over me. Without your arms around me. Without your heartbeat against my ear.

The words were on the tip of his tongue, but even drunk, he couldn't say them, knowing that he would hate himself when he sobered up.

Logan was silent on the line.

Andrew wondered if he could guess what he wasn't saying. He wondered if Logan felt as off balance as he did. He doubted it.

Finally, Logan sighed. "You're such a mess."

"I buried my wife today—again. I'm allowed to be a mess."

Thankfully, Logan didn't say that he was sorry. Andrew wasn't sure he wouldn't burst into tears if he did. His eyes were stinging, his throat tight. The worst part was, he wasn't sure *why* he was feeling so sad, lonely, and needy all of a sudden when he hadn't felt that way at the funeral.

"I think you need a therapist," Logan said.

"Fuck you."

"I'm serious," Logan said, his voice grim. "I did notice that you started associating… certain things with comfort a while ago. A good therapist should be able to help you."

Andrew laughed. "And how do you suggest I tell my problem to a therapist? Please help me sleep without a cock in my mouth? You do realize how humiliating it sounds, right?" He cringed, already hating himself for speaking about the elephant in the room.

Logan, the asshole, snorted. "I'm sure they've heard stranger stuff."

Andrew scoffed and said nothing.

The silence stretched, both of them just breathing into the phone like two weirdos. But he couldn't make himself hang up. God, he felt like he'd burst into tears if Logan hung up on him.

"I really hate you," he whispered, his voice catching. "How are you so well adjusted already while I'm such a mess?"

There was no response for a while.

A breath, then another.

Logan said stiffly, "I wouldn't be calling you in the middle of the night if I were well adjusted."

"I think that was an insult, but I'm too drunk to get offended." Andrew wished it were true. He might be drunk, but Logan's words stabbed something deep inside of him, stabbed and *twisted*. No one needed him. No one wanted him. No one wanted to need him.

It was fine. Fine. He didn't want to need Logan, either.

Logan sighed. "Drink some water and go to sleep, Andrew."

"Don't tell me what to do," he said, even though he was already getting up to go to the mini-bar. He opened a water bottle and drank as much as he could without feeling sick, the phone still pressed to his ear. He was irrationally afraid that Logan would hang up on him, and that fear creeped the hell out of him. He really was messed up in the head, wasn't he?

Feeling tired, Andrew climbed back into the bed and lay on his side.

"Now sleep."

"I don't need you to tell me that," Andrew mumbled, just to be contrary. *I don't need you to sleep*, he wanted to say, but it kind of felt like too much of a lie.

Logan made an irritated noise. "Then why did you want my number?"

Andrew said nothing to that, turning onto his stomach and hugging his pillow.

"Don't hang up," he ordered. *Pleaded.*
God, he'd never felt so pathetic.
There was silence on the line.
"I won't," Logan said at last.
Andrew breathed out, relaxing a little.
He didn't even notice falling asleep.

Chapter 15

The hangover the next morning wasn't as bad as the ball of humiliation that had settled in Andrew's stomach ever since he'd woken up. Fuck, had he really gotten drunk enough to go look for Logan? Like some kind of pathetic stalker? Ugh. And then he'd basically begged Logan not to hang up on him. Double ugh.

"Stupid," Andrew whispered, staring at the ceiling of the room.

The room in Logan's hotel. Just great.

If life could give him one blessing, he would have forgotten what happened last night, but nope, he remembered the mortifying phone conversation with perfect clarity. It figured.

He considered getting up and going to the office, but it wasn't like he was needed there. He wasn't needed anywhere.

The thought just made him feel sorrier for himself, and he hated it, hated feeling so weak and pathetic. He refused to be that pathetic.

Andrew forced himself to get out of bed, take a shower, and go outside. He might not be needed anywhere, but it didn't mean he should let himself sink into a well of depression. He should at least take a walk, be around other people, and hopefully become a functional human being instead of a… whatever mess he was now.

It was easier said than done.

The longer he spent outside, around all the *noise*, around all those people, the more anxious he became. He hadn't known it was possible to feel so alone on a busy street, but apparently it was. No, "alone" was the wrong word. He felt like he was some kind of alien from another planet, like he couldn't connect to all these people at all. He couldn't understand them, he didn't want to be around them, and the more he stayed around them, the harder his heart beat, his anxiety rising and transforming into a panic.

He returned to his hotel room, feeling mentally wrung out and physically shaky. He plopped down onto the bed and dropped his head into his hands, feeling defeated and freaked out.

What was wrong with him? Had he developed some kind of agoraphobia? He didn't… He didn't think so. The thought of being outside didn't really make him anxious. He just didn't like all the noise and people and—it was too much. God, the island had really fucked him up, hadn't it?

A knock on the door made him lift his head.

"Enter," he said listlessly. It was likely a maid wanting to clean the room.

It wasn't a maid.

It was Logan.

It felt like everything stopped, the world coming to an abrupt halt.

Andrew stared at him, wide-eyed, his mouth going slack.

Thud-thud, thud-thud, thud-thud-thud, his heart beat in his chest, as though trying to escape it.

Logan closed the door, leaned back against it, and stared back, his dark eyes bottomless.

Andrew had to grip the bedspread in his fists to stop himself from doing something stupid.

Something stupid like launching himself at Logan and clinging to him like a monkey.

"What are you doing here?" Andrew managed, glaring. At least he hoped he was glaring and not staring at him hungrily.

Logan raised his eyebrows, his inscrutable expression contradicting the stiff, tightly coiled tension in his body. He looked like he'd put on some weight. He looked good. Definitely more put together than Andrew was feeling. But then again, it wasn't a high bar to clear.

"This is my hotel," Logan said. "And you were the one who came here looking for me."

Andrew felt blood rush to his face. "I thought you were in New York."

Some emotion flashed across Logan's face and then it was gone, too quickly for Andrew to recognize it.

"I was," he said curtly.

Andrew moistened his lips with his tongue, unsure.

Silence fell between them, charged with something terribly familiar. It felt *awful* but also incredibly comforting. Easy.

To his utter disgust, Andrew felt more like himself than he had in weeks. The restless, maddening anxiety under his skin—the sense of wrongness—was almost entirely gone. He just looked at Logan, and everything felt right with the world. *But he's still too far—need him closer—why is he so far away—*

Andrew clutched the bedspread tighter. Fuck, if he could bleach his own brain, he would. Seriously, what was wrong with him?

"Maybe I do need a therapist," he said with a hoarse chuckle.

Logan's expression remained sour and unhappy.

He didn't ask for clarification. In fact, he looked as though he'd rather be anywhere but there, something faintly irritated about him. Except his dark eyes remained fixed on Andrew with frightening intensity.

"You didn't get a haircut," Logan said.

Andrew blinked. He cocked his head to the side, confused. His haircut, or lack thereof, was the last thing he'd expected Logan to comment on.

Frowning, he ran a hand through his hair. It really was long now, almost touching his neck in messy curls. It probably looked like a bird's nest. He really should get a haircut.

He'd always cut his hair short for Vivian. It wasn't that she hadn't liked him with longer hair—the curls just made him look younger, making the age difference between them more pronounced. Andrew knew it had made his wife uncomfortable and self-conscious, hence the short haircut. But with Vivian gone, he hadn't bothered. Self-grooming had been the last thing on his mind.

Catching his bottom lip between his teeth, Andrew looked back at him carefully. "Why are you here?"

Logan shrugged, shoving his hands into the pockets of his dark slacks, which drew Andrew's gaze to—

He tore his eyes away, his ears turning hot, his mouth dry.

"I was in the area," Logan said tersely.

"You just said you were in New York," Andrew pointed out.

Logan glared at him, his expression dark, a muscle ticking in his jaw. His very tanned jaw. His neck still looked bronzed against that light blue shirt and—

Andrew dropped his eyes, balling the bedspread in his fists.

"I didn't tell you my room number," he said, just to say something. Anything. "You stalked me."

"It's hardly stalking when you stalked me first."

Andrew's gaze snapped up. He glowered at Logan. "Your hotel's address is publicly available information. There was no stalking involved."

Logan straightened from his slouch against the door, and Andrew's heart started beating faster. He sat very still as Logan approached him.

He stopped in front of Andrew and looked down at him. "Let's drop the bullshit," he said quietly. His hand— large, strong, so familiar—touched the curly strand by Andrew's temple.

Andrew couldn't *breathe*. He could only look into Logan's chocolate-brown eyes, like a rabbit caught in a hunter's trap. "B-bullshit?" he whispered, almost shaking with the effort to keep still and not lean into the touch.

"You all but begged me to come," Logan said, his expression half-disgusted, half-hungry. "You need me."

Andrew scowled at him, his face uncomfortably warm. "No more than you need me."

Logan's lips thinned into a line, but he didn't deny it. He *didn't deny* it.

"It's a side effect of depending on each other for nine months," Logan said, irritation lacing his words. "It's codependency."

Andrew nodded, in full agreement with him on that.

"It'll pass," Logan said, his hand burying in Andrew's hair. "I already had a meeting with a therapist. She said it's nothing incurable. We just need to relearn how to function normally and keep a healthy distance…"

Logan was still saying something, but Andrew couldn't focus anymore.

His whole world seemed to narrow to that hand in his hair, fingers raking against his scalp, the touch sending shivers of pleasure through his body. It wasn't enough.

A whine left his lips and he tipped forward, pressing his face against Logan's hard stomach. Logan's shirt was in the way and he pushed it up with trembling fingers until his face was pressed against that warm, glorious skin. God. God.

Logan was rigid against him, his abdominal muscles twitching against his face. Andrew rubbed his cheek against Logan's happy trail, all the tension and frustration of the past few weeks bleeding out of him. He *breathed*, for what felt like the first time in weeks. In and out. In and out. Much better. He felt so much better. He felt intoxicated. So, so good.

"For fuck's sake," Logan gritted out above him. "This is exactly what we shouldn't be doing."

But his hand was still buried in Andrew's hair and it wasn't pushing him away, not even when Andrew drunkenly nuzzled his way lower, mouthing at the bulge under Logan's pants, *needing* it.

"Christ," Logan breathed out, his hand already working on his belt. "All right, I guess one more time won't make a difference." He unzipped his fly and his hard cock sprang out of it, hitting Andrew's face.

Andrew stared at it hungrily and parted his lips, silently inviting it inside.

Logan groaned and pushed his cock into his mouth in one hard thrust.

God yes.

Everything after that was a blur of gut-wrenching pleasure and need. Andrew was only vaguely aware that he was making obscene sounds and moaning around that cock like a cock-hungry cocksucker, but he couldn't bring himself to care. He felt so good.

Some awareness slipped back into Andrew when he felt Logan's hands gripping his face and holding it still as he fucked his mouth harder. He allowed it, his brain too intoxicated and hazy to think. He loved it, loved being used by Logan, loved being just a warm mouth for his cock. It felt right. He felt needed. Essential.

He slipped his hand into his sweatpants and started stroking his own aching cock, but he could barely focus on it. All his focus was on the familiar cock fucking his mouth, the way it bumped against the back of his throat, making him gag a little, how good it felt to have his lips stretched wide around the thick length. The taste of him was so familiar. So right. He'd missed it so much.

"Wait," Logan ground out, pulling his cock out of Andrew's mouth.

Andrew made a protesting noise, his brain unable to comprehend anything. He let Logan push him back onto the bed and arrange their bodies so Logan's face was above his cock. He gasped when Logan's hot mouth wrapped around his aching cock, but the pleasure felt secondary to his *need* to suck Logan's. He guided Logan's cock back into his mouth, moaning in relief as it started fucking his mouth again. This was all he wanted. This was all he'd needed. This cock, the taste of it, the way it filled his mouth.

When Logan came, Andrew swallowed his jizz greedily but kept sucking—until Logan hissed in discomfort and pulled out. "Oversensitive," he said, before going back to sucking Andrew's cock.

Andrew buried his face in Logan's crotch, drowning in his scent, Logan's mouth hot and tight around his cock. God.

Logan stroked his balls, and Andrew came with a muffled moan, shaking and panting.

He floated on the cloud of *pleasure-good-right* for a long time. He whined and grabbed Logan's arm when he started pulling away. *Don't go.*

"Okay," Logan said.

The mattress dipped. Logan stretched out next to him on his back. Andrew immediately rolled on top of him. Logan made an annoyed noise but didn't push him off.

Taking it as permission, Andrew unbuttoned Logan's shirt and put his face on the other man's pecs, enjoying the familiar sensation of Logan's sparse chest hair tickling his cheek. His body went boneless, a feeling of warm contentment spreading through him.

"Just this time," Andrew mumbled. "We'll go to a therapist tomorrow."

Logan sighed, his hand setting on Andrew's back and pulling him closer. "Yes. Tomorrow."

Chapter 16

Logan stared at the man sleeping on his chest and wondered how it was possible to feel so relaxed and at ease when he had clearly lost his mind.

This hadn't been the plan. He had arrived at the hotel to *check up* on Andrew, not to fall into the same rabbit hole again. The guy had sounded like a mess on the phone, and Logan had intended to just check up on him and then go on with his life.

Right, said a sardonic voice at the back of his mind. *You're as bad as he is, if not worse.*

Running a hand over his face, Logan sighed. Yeah, maybe. If he were honest with himself, being away from Andrew had been… frustrating. These past weeks he'd constantly felt distracted, his body crawling with agitation. He was too used to sleeping wrapped around Andrew, too used to taking care of him. Logan had expected—hoped— that with the return to the normal world, his former independent habits would be back, but so far it wasn't happening. Or maybe the need to be needed by Andrew had become too deeply ingrained into him.

Either way, what happened last night was a mistake. A mistake he shouldn't make again. As long as he didn't make it again, it should be fine. It was like quitting smoking: stopping completely wasn't easy, but as long as he didn't make a habit out of it, it was still possible to quit.

Isn't it the same thing you told yourself back on the island?

Carefully pushing the uncomfortable thought away, Logan studied Andrew's sleeping face, his brows furrowing when he noticed again how thin it was. Andrew was all lips and eyes now, his face almost gaunt. He was still ridiculously lovely, but this thinness didn't look healthy. It wasn't just his face; he'd definitely lost a lot of weight overall.

As if feeling his gaze, Andrew mumbled something sleepily and shifted. Those large, pretty eyes opened. They seemed more blue than green this morning. They blinked at Logan owlishly before closing again. "Is it morning already?" he muttered into Logan's chest, rubbing his cheek against it like a sleepy kitten.

Logan's stomach tightened, a funny feeling twisting it. It wasn't an unpleasant feeling, just an unsettling one.

"Yes. Get off me. I need to go."

Andrew went very still for a moment.

Then he rolled off him and sat up.

Logan sat up, too.

They just stared at each other for a moment.

"You're all skin and bones," Logan said. "Have you been eating at all? You weren't this thin on the island."

Andrew shrugged vaguely. It could mean anything.

When Logan continued looking at him, Andrew said, "I forget."

"You forget," Logan repeated flatly. "You forget to eat."

Andrew wouldn't meet his eyes.

Logan sighed.

He reached for the phone on the nightstand and contacted reception. "Good morning. Breakfast for two, please."

After a moment's pause, the receptionist said quickly, "Of course, Mr. McCall."

Andrew was glaring at Logan when he turned back to him. "Why did you do that?" he said, two spots of color appearing on his cheekbones. "Now they're going to think that—that…"

"That you sucked my dick and I stayed the night?" Logan said, very dryly.

"I didn't suck your dick," Andrew said, avoiding his gaze as he straightened his clothes. "I'm not gay."

Logan snorted a laugh. "Of course not. You just like having your mouth fucked. With a cock."

The withering look Andrew shot him could have set someone on fire. "You're not funny."

"I'm not trying to be," Logan said, heading to the ensuite. He needed a shower.

By the time he returned, clad only in a towel wrapped around his hips, a maid was setting down a tray with breakfast on the table.

She started when she saw Logan, her eyes shooting from him to Andrew, whose face was red again.

"Good morning, Mr. McCall," she said cheerfully, as if there was nothing strange about the situation.

"Good morning," Logan said. "There are no bathrobes in the bathroom. Make sure that's corrected."

The maid flushed. "Of course, Mr. McCall. The only reason we didn't bring them in was because there was a 'do not disturb' sign on the door since Mr. Reyes moved in."

Logan nodded. He didn't bother saying that they should have brought a bathrobe before a new guest checked into the room; making her flustered would accomplish nothing. But he'd have to talk to the manager about this.

Andrew threw him a t-shirt. Logan caught it and slipped into it. It was a little tight around his chest and shoulders but nothing too uncomfortable.

"You may go, Jane," he said, glancing at the maid when he realized that she was still there. "Have someone bring me clothes from my suite."

She nodded and quickly left.

Logan sat down at the table and poured them both coffee. "Sit. Eat."

Andrew scowled but did as he was told. He nibbled the food at first before suddenly attacking it ravenously, as if only now realizing how hungry he was. Christ, it seemed he hadn't eaten in days. He certainly looked it.

Logan watched him eat, trying to place the strange feeling that curled in his gut. It wasn't unfamiliar. It took him a moment to recognize it. It was similar to the primitive satisfaction he derived from watching Andrew enjoy the food he cooked. He liked feeding Andrew. Providing for him.

Cringing on the inside, Logan looked away and focused on his own food.

They ate in silence. It should have probably been uncomfortable, but it actually was the most comfortable Logan had felt in weeks.

Returning home and seeing his family and friends for the first time in nearly a year had felt good, of course, but it had done nothing to erase the uneasy feeling under his skin, as if he'd misplaced something. Now that dissatisfied feeling was gone. He felt completely at ease.

It wasn't that these feelings were completely surprising.

It was probably natural that it would take him time to get used to his normal life.

It was to be expected that he would still feel more comfortable around the person who had been his world for nine months. In time, these feelings should disappear. He just had to give it time—and *stop* feeding the codependency, dammit.

The sound of a ringtone snapped him out of his thoughts. Andrew started, too, before reaching for his phone and staring at it with something like trepidation.

Logan raised his eyebrows. "Someone you don't want to talk to?"

Andrew's face did something weird. "It's my aunt. She raised me."

It hadn't escaped Logan's notice that it wasn't a no.

None of your damn business, he told himself and returned his gaze to his food. He pretended to be engrossed in it as Andrew answered the phone.

"...no, Auntie, I swear I didn't forget... I know I promised to visit you today, and I will, I promise... I had no idea you were expecting me this early—"

The woman on the other end of the line seemed to launch into a tirade.

Andrew listened to it with a resigned, pinched look on his face, his shoulders growing tenser with every moment. He looked... small. Andrew wasn't a small man, but right now "small" was a good word to describe him. He looked small. Like anything could break him. Or something already had.

Logan frowned.

"I'm sorry. I'll be heading out right now," Andrew said at last before ending the call.

He stared at his phone for a moment, a blank look on his face, before springing to his feet.

"I have to go," he said, without looking at Logan.

"I promised my aunt that I'd visit her today, and apparently she's been expecting me for hours."

"You need a ride?" Logan said before he could stop himself.

Andrew's brows furrowed. "Do you have a car? I thought you lived in New York?"

Logan looked away. "I drove here," he said curtly. Andrew didn't need to know that he couldn't sleep after hearing his voice, thinking about him and obsessing. He hadn't even noticed at first that he was driving toward Boston, and then it was too late to turn back. Or so he had told himself.

"Oh," Andrew said. "Okay, then."

"Go take a shower and get dressed."

Andrew rolled his eyes with a long-suffering look. "Fuck you. I don't need you to tell me what to do. I'm capable of functioning on my own, you know."

"Are you?" Logan said quietly. "Are you okay, Drew?"

Andrew's jaw clenched, something almost fragile in his eyes. He looked at Logan uncertainly and said nothing.

Logan's hands twitched toward him, but his ill-advised urge to comfort was interrupted by the knock on the door. Good timing.

Logan went to open it and thanked the maid for bringing him some clothes. He dropped the towel and started dressing unhurriedly as Andrew disappeared into the ensuite.

He was checking his emails on his phone when Andrew finally emerged from the bathroom, already dressed. He went still, looking at Logan with a strange expression on his face.

"What?" Logan said.

Andrew shook his head, rubbing the back of his neck. "Nothing," he said, his lips twisted into something that wasn't quite a smile. "I'm still not used to you being all…"

"Dressed?" Logan said with a snort.

"Yeah," Andrew said, laughing a little. "It's really throwing me off."

They left the room together.

Logan ignored the curious looks that followed them everywhere, forcing himself to relax. After the solitude of the island, he was still struggling to adjust to having so many people stare at him all the time. A sideways glance at Andrew confirmed that the other man was faring much worse: there was so much tension in the way Andrew was carrying himself it looked like he might snap any moment, his eyes darting around nervously.

Frowning, Logan laid a hand on Andrew's back. He'd half-expected Andrew to jump away from him skittishly, but instead, some of the tension seemed to bleed out of Andrew's body. Andrew moved closer to him, walking so close that their shoulders bumped.

Logan's frown deepened. He glanced down at Andrew's hand. His fingers were clenching and unclenching.

It was a relief to finally reach the car.

Andrew sagged back into the passenger seat, running a hand over his face with a sigh. "Fuck."

Fuck indeed. Logan hadn't thought it was this bad.

He started the car, considering how to broach the subject while Andrew was putting his aunt's address into his GPS.

"All these people… it seems a little too much sometimes, doesn't it?" he said at last.

"Don't patronize me," Andrew said without much heat in his voice.

"I'm not patronizing you. You think it's easy for me?"

Andrew shot him a sour look, his full lips pursing.

Logan fixed his gaze on the road.

"You're not a mess," Andrew said. "Not like me."

"I feel uncomfortable around people, too."

"But it isn't as hard for you," Andrew stated.

"No, it isn't."

"*Why?*" Andrew said, his voice full of bewilderment and misery.

Logan had to choose his words carefully. "I've gotten the impression that you always relied on your wife to be a steady presence for you. Your rock. You relied on her support a lot. Is that correct?"

Andrew didn't answer immediately.

"Maybe," he said at last.

"And then on the island…" Logan trailed off, unsure how to put it in a way that wouldn't offend him.

Andrew snorted. "I used you like my comfort blanket."

Smiling wryly, Logan said, "More of a teddy bear or a pacifier."

"Maybe," Andrew said with an uncomfortable chuckle. "So what? Get to the point."

"My point is, it seems you're used to someone grounding you. You don't do well without it. Combined with the issue of adjusting to the real world, it's understandable that you're having a harder time."

Andrew didn't say anything, turning his face away to stare out the window.

Logan suppressed a sigh.

They remained silent for the rest of the ride.

When the car stopped in front of a nice, picturesque house in the suburbs, Andrew didn't move to get out of the car. He was staring at the house with a strange expression, his face pale and his hands fidgeting with his seatbelt.

"It's that one, right?" Logan said.

Andrew nodded woodenly, unbuckled the seatbelt, and slowly got out of the car. He took a few steps before freezing again.

Logan frowned and got out of the car, too.

Rounding it, he touched Andrew's shoulder. "What's—"

Andrew whirled around and grabbed him by his shirt. "I—I need— Don't leave." He flushed, a look of frustration and mortification flashing across his face, but his blue-green eyes remained wide and pleading.

Fucking hell.

"Okay," he said, putting his own hands over Andrew's and carefully forcing them to relax their grip on his shirt. He rubbed Andrew's knuckles after that and squeezed them, watching the other man's eyes glaze over.

Christ.

Logan clenched his jaw, his boxers suddenly a little too tight. Fixing his mind on the most disgusting things he could think of, Logan guided Andrew toward the front door with a steady hand on his back, ignoring the voice at the back of his mind that kept saying, *What are you doing?*

The woman that opened the door didn't look much like her nephew. She was short and plump where Andrew was tall and fit, their curly brown hair the only thing they had in common.

She was already frowning when she opened the door, and her frown only deepened when she saw Logan. Her lips pursed briefly before stretching into a polite smile.

"Good morning. I didn't expect Andrew to bring a guest. You must be Logan, correct?"

Logan smiled amiably and engaged her in meaningless small talk, all the while observing her and her nephew.

Andrew barely seemed capable of looking at her directly. His body was so full of tension it was painful to look at. He seemed to be torn between sticking close to Logan and putting as much distance between them as possible.

It didn't take Logan long to guess why. Although the woman was unfailingly polite, it soon became obvious that she didn't approve of her nephew's association with him. And since Logan was virtually a stranger to her, there was only one thing she could disapprove of: his sexuality wasn't exactly secret. Now some things about Andrew were starting to make a lot of sense.

The conversation over the tea table was excruciatingly uncomfortable. Andrew barely spoke besides "Yes, Auntie" and "No, Auntie," while Rebecca made her opinions known on a wide variety of topics that ranged from her nephew's "disastrous hair" to his state of unemployment.

"You must take your company back," she said sharply. "You absolutely must. Those people—the Rutledges—had no right to take away your company and hand it to someone else! You have worked for it for years, and you own ten percent of the company now that your wife is gone. You can't just let them kick you out like a useless thing—"

"Yes, Auntie," Andrew said, looking like he'd rather be anywhere but there.

And on and on it went.

By the time they finished their tea, Logan was this close to strangling that woman. The worst part was, she seemed to mean well, but her overbearing attitude was unbearable. Logan couldn't imagine growing up under the woman's care. Fuck, it really explained so much about Andrew. So damn much.

Although Rebecca all but ignored Logan, her displeasure about his presence in her house was glaringly obvious. Logan could never stand people like her: people who considered themselves too well mannered to be openly homophobic but who treated gay people with barely hidden disdain. No wonder Andrew had been such a bigot: the guy craved approval and praise so much, he'd probably subconsciously suppressed any "abnormal" leanings just to please this woman, and then overcompensated.

It pissed Logan off. He wished he'd had the willpower to say no when Andrew had asked him to stay. He wished he had remained oblivious to this. He wished… Fuck, he wished he'd had some self-control and remained in New York instead of all but running here just because Andrew had sounded upset over the phone. Damn it all.

Sometimes ignorance *was* bliss. It was bad enough that he had no self-control when it came to Andrew and couldn't keep it in his pants. He didn't need to feel sorry for him on top of that. Or *protective* of him.

But no matter what Logan told himself, he did feel it. The longer he watched Rebecca and her nephew, the harder it was to keep his mouth shut and not to snap at her to mind her own business. He didn't like how small Andrew looked in this house.

He didn't like the way his shoulders were hunched defensively, the way his confidence seemed to completely disappear the longer they were there.

It rubbed Logan the wrong way, made him want to put himself between Andrew and this woman and *growl*. It was pure instinct, no matter how ridiculous and bizarre it was, an instinct that was becoming harder to suppress with every minute.

Finally, he stood and said tersely, "Thanks for the tea, but we should go." He grabbed Andrew's wrist and pulled him to his feet, ignoring the startled, wide-eyed look Andrew shot him.

Rebecca looked at Logan for the first time in a while, her lips flattened into a line. "We? Truth be told, I'm a little lost. I'm not sure why you and my nephew are still associating, Logan. I understand that you were forced to coexist on the island in order to survive, but surely continuing such association is… inadvisable. Andrew needs to move on with his life, leave the island in the past."

Logan smiled at her, aware that it wasn't a very nice smile.

It probably looked a little feral. He didn't care; he was too pissed off to care that he was being rude. It didn't matter that he'd come to similar conclusions himself—that he needed to keep his distance from the mess of a human being Andrew was—he was too annoyed now to agree with this woman on anything.

"We became close on the island," he said, taking perverse pleasure in watching her frown in distaste. "After living in each other's pockets for so long, I'm afraid now I can't even sleep without him drooling all over my chest."

Rebecca flushed, then paled, and shot her nephew an appalled look.

Andrew's face was red as a tomato. He opened his mouth and then closed it without saying anything, his wide-eyed gaze unable to meet his aunt's.

For a moment, Logan felt a twinge of guilt, but it wasn't as though he was admitting something obscene. Rebecca would probably just laugh at his words if he weren't gay. It was her own bigotry that was making her assume gay men were incapable of friendship and affection. And she obviously thought Andrew shouldn't have let a gay man anywhere near him.

"Come on," Logan said, laying a hand on Andrew's nape and steering him toward the door.

Andrew didn't resist, just mumbled a goodbye to his aunt. She didn't say anything.

As soon as they were outside, it was as though Andrew was a completely different person. He whirled around and glared at Logan. "What the hell was that?"

Logan's lips twitched. He much preferred this Andrew to the doormat he had become around his aunt. He shrugged. "What? I simply told her the truth. Or was it supposed to be a secret? You did drool on my chest."

Andrew huffed, his lips pursing, before he stomped toward Logan's car.

Logan followed him at a more sedate pace, feeling more amused than the situation called for. Christ, had he really missed these hissy fits? Was this... *fondness*? Affection?

His smile fading, Logan got into the driver's seat and started the engine. He said, without looking at Andrew, "It was your idea. I had no intention of meeting your bigoted aunt. You all but begged me to come with you."

"I didn't," Andrew said, sounding a little choked up. "I didn't *beg* you. I don't need you."

Logan's lips thinned. He stared at the car in front of them. "Denying it is kind of pointless when all the evidence points to the contrary."

"You arrogant, conceited—! No one forced you to stay and make it look like we're best friends or—or worse."

"Or worse," Logan said flatly. "Will it really be the end of the world if she finds out you're bisexual?"

He'd expected an immediate denial, but it didn't come.

The light turned red, and Logan took the opportunity to look at him.

Andrew was looking down at his own hands, his brows furrowed, a curl falling into his eyes.

"No objections?" Logan said.

"Do you really think…?" Andrew looked up. "You really think I'm bi?"

Logan returned his gaze to the road. "I know you liked to pretend I was forcing you to suck my dick, but surely you don't still think that?"

When silence was the only response, Logan chuckled harshly. "All right, it's none of my business. You're none of my business." Maybe if he repeated it often enough, he might finally start acting like it. God, he couldn't wait.

Silence fell again, thick with something heavy and charged.

It started raining.

Logan's hands clenched on the steering wheel. "Back to the hotel?" he said, his voice harsher than he had intended.

"No," Andrew said after a moment. "I need to relearn how to be around other people. Just… drop me somewhere with a lot of people."

Logan did as he was told, quashing the urge to tell him that it was raining and he'd get soaked. He wasn't Andrew's minder. The guy was a grown man. He could survive a few hours on his own.

He didn't look at Andrew as he got out of the car.

But it was a struggle to wrench his gaze away from the lone figure in the rearview mirror. Andrew looked so small and thin, standing there with his arms crossed defensively over his chest, his head down and his shoulders hunched.

His every instinct screamed to get out of the car, grab Andrew, and tell him that of course he was Logan's business. *Just his.*

Logan swore under his breath and drove away, the tires screeching against the asphalt.

The rain became heavier, as did the ball of anxiety in his stomach.

Chapter 17

Logan spent the afternoon going over their accounts with his hotel manager—and not thinking about Andrew.

He really was none of Logan's business. A repressed "straight" guy who was so deep in denial he couldn't even admit that he wanted Logan should be avoided like the plague. Nothing would ever come out of it. They were nothing to each other. He had no business worrying that Andrew might have had a panic attack somewhere or might be cold after walking around in the rain for hours, or upset and in need of comforting—

Yeah, good job not thinking about him.

Logan was in a shitty mood as he returned to his room that evening. He took a long shower and jerked off *not* thinking about anything or anyone in particular, but it didn't help. He still felt agitated.

The knock on the door both surprised him and didn't.

Clad only in his boxers, Logan went to open it.

Andrew stood on the other side. He was worrying his bottom lip, his shoulders so tense Logan could feel the tension in them with his own skin.

He didn't even blink at seeing Logan nearly naked—but then again, he was used to it.

They just stared at each other for a moment.

Logan should have probably said something. He should have probably told Andrew to fuck off. He should have at least asked Andrew what the hell he thought he was doing.

He did none of those things.

He stepped aside, allowing Andrew to enter the room.

Andrew did.

Logan shut the door, locked it, and walked to the bed. He stretched out on his back and closed his eyes. Andrew turned the lights off. There was the sound of clothes being removed, and then the mattress dipped.

A warm, familiar body curled up on top of him, skin against skin. Andrew pressed his face between Logan's pecs and took a deep, shuddering breath. "Hold me," he whispered.

Logan opened his eyes and stared at the dark ceiling. And then he lifted his arms and wrapped them around Andrew.

A small sound left Andrew's mouth. A whimper. "Tighter."

Logan tightened his arms, their bodies pressing flush against each other, skin to skin, so tightly there wasn't a hair's breadth between them. It was bliss. It was torture. It was everything he had missed and wanted these past weeks. More than the sex—the closeness. The rightness. The exquisite intimacy of holding this person in his arms and feeling at peace with himself and the world. Like two pieces of a puzzle. Two pieces of a puzzle that should have never fit together and yet they had somehow learned to— and now couldn't unlearn it.

"I hate this," Andrew said, his voice wavering.

"I know," Logan said. "Me, too."

He meant it. He hated how right this felt—holding this mess of a human being, this guy who was a total wreck, who was bigoted and beyond repressed but at the same time vulnerable, lonely, and hungry for affection and approval.

"It's like a fucking disease," Andrew said into his chest, barely audibly. "Something empty and wrong inside me. I feel like—like a river without water. The world feels so off without you, and you're the only thing that makes me feel whole."

Christ.

Logan bit the inside of his cheek, his cock so hard it was uncomfortable. Nothing about Andrew's words should have been arousing. Nothing.

"And yet you can't even admit that you want me," Logan said roughly.

Silence.

Logan heaved a sigh. "You should go." He was aware how insincere his voice sounded. It probably wasn't convincing at all, considering that his arms were wrapped tightly around the other man, and his body was rigid with the effort not to grope Andrew all over. Fuck, he wanted him. He wanted to flip Andrew onto his back and pound this infuriating, confusing mess of a man into the mattress, screw Andrew on his cock until Andrew could feel him against his fucking *heart*. He'd never wanted to fuck, to *possess* anyone more. He'd never felt like he'd explode if he didn't put his cock into someone and mark them up from the inside.

But why shouldn't he?

Maybe he should just fuck Andrew.

Maybe that was exactly what he needed to get him out of his system.

No matter how hard Logan tried to shake the idea off, it refused to go away.

What did they have to lose, really?

Just once. They could do it just once.

Before he could stop himself, he moved his hands lower, slipping them under the waistband of Andrew's boxers. Andrew didn't even tense, which probably spoke volumes of how accustomed to touching each other they were, but fuck, the mere fact that this supposedly straight guy needed him so badly that even feeling Logan's hands on his ass didn't bother him at all… it was like a heady drug. The worst kind of drug.

Logan had never considered himself a possessive man. He'd always thought possessiveness didn't belong in the modern world. But this submissiveness, the way Andrew allowed Logan to touch him anywhere he wanted, brought out primitive instincts that were more appropriate for a caveman. *Mine*, they whispered, like poison in his mind. *Mine mine mine.*

Andrew's cheeks were silky smooth and just the right size, plump but firm. Logan kneaded them greedily for a while, enjoying the way they felt in his hands, the way Andrew allowed him this without any protest.

Finally, Logan reached out to the nightstand and retrieved the lube from the drawer.

Andrew tensed only when Logan pressed a slick finger between his cheeks.

"What are you doing?"

"Isn't it obvious?" Logan said, massaging his hole with his fingers.

Andrew was twitching, tense—but still not pulling away. "You aren't—you aren't fucking me," he said, but he didn't sound all that sure. "Stop."

Logan ignored him, knowing how it went. If Andrew truly wanted him to stop, he would use his safeword.

He pushed a finger into the tight hole, and Andrew inhaled sharply. "N-no," he stuttered. "Don't."

"All you have to do is say your safeword: funeral," Logan said. "And I'll stop. But your 'no' and 'stop' don't mean shit. We both know it."

"No," Andrew said. "Stop—don't—ah—"

"You like this," Logan stated, slipping another finger into him. He found Andrew's prostate and stroked it, drawing muffled moans from the guy on his chest. "Say it."

"I'm not—ah—"

"Not gay?" Logan said, working his fingers in and out of him. Christ, he was so fucking tight. "Then say the word, and I'll stop. I'll pull my fingers out and we can pretend you hated this. Or…"

Andrew was silent, but his silence was tense, questioning.

"Or I can put you on your back and fuck you with my cock," Logan said hoarsely, stabbing his fingers against Andrew's prostate. Andrew shuddered. Logan smiled and massaged the bump in circular motions. Andrew let out a long moan, moving his hips involuntarily.

Logan put his free hand on Andrew's lower back, pressing their bare stomachs together. "Just imagine, Drew," he said, his voice so deep and husky it didn't even sound like his own. "You said I'm the only thing that makes you feel whole. Imagine having me inside of you physically too. It'll feel so good. My cock moving inside you. My come filling your stomach. Me—in you. So deep there's nothing between us."

Andrew made a small noise and shook his head, but his hips kept moving, pushing back onto Logan's fingers as if of their own volition. His parted lips were mouthing Logan's chest before latching onto his nipple. Groaning, Logan pushed a third finger in, stretching the tight, warm passage that enveloped his slick fingers like a glove.

Fuck, his cock ached, eager to replace his fingers.

Unable to wait anymore, Logan rolled them, pushing Andrew under him. Andrew made a desperate sound when Logan's fingers slipped out of him, but Logan was already pressing his cockhead against the slicked hole. At the back of his mind, the last remnants of his rationality tried to remind him of things like condoms, but he couldn't stop. He wanted. He felt like he'd explode if he didn't get his cock into this man right now.

So he pushed inside in one hard thrust, and they both groaned. Andrew was so tight it was almost painful, but Christ, it felt so good, as if he'd finally reached his life goal, the relief so immense Logan nearly came on the spot.

"You asshole," Andrew breathed out, his body tense under him. "You couldn't do it slower?"

No, he couldn't. He'd been wanting this for months.

Logan forced his eyes open and stared at the dark spot that was Andrew. He suddenly wished he could see what he looked like right now, spread out under him, full of his cock.

But maybe it was a good thing he couldn't see it. It was bad enough that he was letting his cock do the thinking—again. Knowing what Andrew *looked* like on his cock was an image he'd rather live without.

Logan closed his eyes again and started thrusting. He just needed to get it over with. The sooner he came, the sooner he'd get this guy out from under his skin.

He thrust and thrust and thrust, his fingers digging into Andrew's hipbones, holding him still as he took his pleasure. The other man was quiet at first—or at least was trying to be—but soon enough the occasional muffled whimpers and gasps turned into continuous moans that grew progressively louder.

Fuck, he was a *slut* for it, his hips gyrating on Logan's cock as if he had been born for it. And the infuriating part was, Andrew was still trying to pretend he wasn't loving this. "Stop—ah—don't—ah fuck!"

It made Logan absolutely crazy with a mix of want and rage. He shoved Andrew onto his hands and knees and slammed back into him. Andrew *keened*, lifting his ass higher, pushing back onto his cock.

"Still want me to stop?" he growled into Andrew's ear, fucking him from behind, hard and fast.

"Yes—ah—no—don't—harder."

Logan bit him on the shoulder and fucked him harder. The bed was squeaking under them, the headboard banging against the wall, the noises leaving their mouths completely inhuman now. Like animals rutting together, for the sake of sating their instincts, a primitive need that couldn't be denied.

Logan had no idea how long it lasted. He was only vaguely aware of Andrew coming first, untouched, just from his cock—and fuck, the mere thought was like a powerful aphrodisiac, and Logan came, too, with a loud groan that would have been embarrassing in any other circumstances.

He fell on top of Andrew, burying his face in his damp nape. He breathed deeply. *Mine.* It was bliss. He'd never felt better in his life.

He drifted off, still buried inside him.

Chapter 18

The first rays of morning sun filtered in through the curtains.

Andrew stared at them unseeingly.

There was a heavy arm wrapped around his waist. There was a firm male body behind him, pressed flush against his back. A warm breath was tickling the sensitive skin at his nape.

All of it was so familiar and—God help him—*comforting*. Andrew had woken up half an hour ago but still hadn't managed to force himself to pull out of Logan's arms. Every cell of his body seemed to sing with contentment, his traitorous body refusing to part from its other half. *Its other half.* Jesus fucking Christ. His own thoughts freaked him out. Though his thoughts still weren't as freaky as the fact that he had let another man stick his cock into his ass and make him come so hard that he'd blacked out and slept like the proverbial baby.

Logan's cock was still in his ass. And it was hard again.

He had another man's erection in his ass.

Andrew's brain kept fixating on that, hysteria bubbling in his chest. Rationally, he knew there wasn't much of a difference between being fucked in the mouth and being fucked in the ass—both acts should have been equally wrong, and yet… taking it up the ass seemed more… final. More emasculating. Andrew could explain away his need to suck Logan's cock with a need for comfort, with some kind of weird Stockholm Syndrome thing, but *this*… This was far worse.

He hadn't allowed Logan to fuck him even back on the island. He had no excuse at all now.

He should get out of the bed before Logan woke up and got the wrong idea that Andrew had liked what he'd done to him.

The wrong idea? a voice said at the back of his mind snidely. *As if you weren't moaning like a slut when he fucked you?*

Andrew blushed. Just remembering it made him shiver. Andrew glared down in betrayal at his erection and carefully tried to extract himself out of Logan's arms. But all his squirming only managed to press Logan's cock even deeper into him, bumping against his prostate. Andrew moaned and shoved his face into the pillow to muffle the noise. Fuck!

Logan mumbled something in his sleep and rolled them onto their stomachs. He stopped moving again and his breathing evened out, except now Andrew was completely pinned under his body, his hole speared on Logan's hard cock.

God.

His traitorous cock seemed to only become harder, arousal and pleasure spreading through his body in warm waves. The feeling of being under Logan's firm, heavy body, unable to move and utterly helpless, was doing something strange to him. It felt so achingly right, to be blocked from the rest of the world by Logan's bulk, having him on him and around him, as if the two of them were the only thing that existed. And having Logan *inside* him, on the deepest level one could have a man, it was… it did things to him. It fed the needy, hungry thing inside him. He wanted more.

When did you turn into such a cock slut?

Andrew flushed, feeling embarrassed, confused, and irritated with himself, but fuck, it felt so good. Having a cock in his ass had no business feeling so good. A man shouldn't want to be *taken* by another man. It was wrong. He shouldn't want this. It was so damn pathetic. Logan was asleep, for fuck's sake. Andrew shouldn't want to move his hips and fuck himself on that fat cock—except it was exactly what he wanted. Shame washed over him. It was as though Logan had awoken an insatiable creature inside him, one that just wanted more, more, and more.

Logan mumbled something in his sleep, and his hips started thrusting shallowly.

Andrew bit his bottom lip hard, swallowing a moan. He should stop Logan. He should shove him off. He should—

He moaned into the pillow as Logan's rhythm increased. God, he really was a cock slut. He could only hope Logan wouldn't wake up. He wouldn't be able to look him in the eye.

"Morning," Logan said into his ear, his voice husky from sleep.

Andrew wished for the ground to open and swallow him. He didn't say anything, hoping Logan would think he was asleep.

With a soft snort, Logan continued moving. Thrusting.

"I know you aren't asleep," he said, nuzzling into the side of Andrew's face, his hips moving faster, the obscene slaps of skin against skin filling the room. "You can stop pretending now."

Andrew remained quiet, biting the pillow to muffle any noise.

Logan, the asshole, had the nerve to laugh.

"I can see how red your ears are," he said conversationally, biting his earlobe. "You're blushing, Drew."

Andrew's chest felt funny—full, and warm, and something else. Thankfully, Logan's next thrust shifted his attention back to the cock in his ass. It rubbed against that spot in him again, and Andrew couldn't swallow his moan this time.

Logan went still.

"No," Andrew whined before he could stop himself.

"Ask," Logan said into his ear. "I'm not playing the game today. You'll have to ask for it this time. Or I won't give you my cock."

"I hate you," Andrew grumbled, shaking with impatience. God, he wanted Logan to *move*. He wanted thrusting. He wanted to be fucked.

"I'm waiting, Drew," Logan said nipping the back of his neck, his hips infuriatingly still. "Say 'fuck me.' It's easy. You know you want to."

Andrew opened his eyes and glared at the headboard. "I won't."

"Okay," Logan said, starting to pull out.

"No," Andrew bit off. He breathed in shakily. "I need you."

Logan shuddered. "You aren't playing fair, damn you."

Andrew smiled a little. He wasn't an idiot. He knew how much Logan liked when he said it. "I need you," he whispered again, squeezing the cock in him. "Need you."

With a growl, Logan snapped. He resumed fucking him, hard and fast.

Andrew couldn't stop his moans anymore. The mattress was bouncing with the force of Logan's thrusts, and the cock moving in him felt so unbelievably good that tears sprang to Andrew's eyes. His *ah, ah, ahs* became so embarrassingly loud that he could only hope the walls were soundproof.

It took him only a few minutes to come, shaking and groaning. He lay, boneless and overwhelmed, in a pool of his own jizz, as Logan sought his orgasm.

When it was over, Andrew rolled Logan onto his back and sprawled on top of him in his favorite position, laying his head over Logan's heart.

Logan's arms wrapped around him, and Andrew allowed himself a small smile against Logan's chest.

He had no idea what they were doing, but right now he felt too good to care.

He felt perfect. Whole.

Chapter 19

The day passed in a blur of sex and *Logan Logan Logan*. They dozed, fucked, dozed, and then fucked again. Andrew felt high, his senses overstimulated, his body one raw nerve of pleasure. It felt like a dream. It felt like a descent into madness. Like falling into an ocean and voluntarily drowning.

He fell asleep at some point, exhausted and sated.

He dreamed of the plane crash.

He dreamed of screams, fear, and the feeling of utter helplessness. He dreamed of shaking Vivian's still body, begging her to wake up. *Why wouldn't she wake up?* Part of him realized that it was a dream, that he'd had this nightmare countless times already. Vivian wouldn't wake up, because she was dead. Logan would tell him that in a moment.

But Logan remained quiet this time.

Confused, he turned away from Vivian and stumbled back in shock. Logan was still in his seat, his neck at an unnatural angle. His dark eyes were blank. Lifeless.

Andrew woke up with a start, a scream caught in his throat.

His heart beating erratically, he looked around. The room was empty.

Wild panic gripped him.

He stumbled out of the bed, looking around in a daze. Where was he?

The door.

He grabbed the door handle, pushed it open, and stepped out of the room. Bright lights from the hall blinded him for a moment.

When his gaze focused, it fell on the tall man nearby. The man's back was to him, but Andrew would recognize it anywhere.

His relief was so strong his knees nearly buckled. He must have made some noise, because Logan turned around and froze.

It took Andrew's sleep-frazzled brain a moment to understand why.

Logan wasn't alone. He had been speaking to two men, one of whom Andrew vaguely recognized as the hotel's manager. They all were finely dressed — while Andrew very much wasn't. He was only in his boxers.

Andrew flushed. He probably looked a sight: his hair a bird's nest, his body nearly naked. And he'd just emerged out of *Logan's* suite, probably leaving little doubt about what they had been doing there, considering his state of undress.

The manager's face went carefully blank, while the other stranger wasn't quite as successful at hiding his shock. He'd likely recognized Andrew as the widower whose wife's funeral had been a few days ago. Just great. Fucking fantastic.

Suppressing the cowardly urge to run back into the room and slam the door shut—it was a little too late for that—Andrew found himself frozen, unsure what to do, hysteria and embarrassment warring inside his chest. What should he do? How soon would the rumors spread?

His eyes locked with Logan's inscrutable dark eyes.

After a moment, Logan walked back to him, shrugging out of his suit jacket. He draped it over Andrew's shoulders, the jacket big enough to cover Andrew's thighs too. "Sorry, I should have left you a change of clothes," Logan said, his voice loud enough to reach the other men's ears. "The coffee completely ruined yours, I'm afraid."

Andrew blinked at him stupidly before realizing what Logan was attempting to do. He was giving him a somewhat plausible explanation for his state of undress. He was giving him a way out.

The rush of gratitude that washed over him was nearly overwhelming.

Andrew nodded numbly, feeling relieved, grateful, and—

But as soon as Logan stepped back, the panic was back. His hand shot out and grabbed Logan's wrist—he barely stopped himself from grabbing his hand. *Don't go.*

Logan looked back at him, something like surprise flashing across his face. His dark eyes were a little softer now.

"I'm not leaving," he said, his voice quieter. "I'll be back in a few minutes. I promise."

Andrew felt as though his face was burning. Was he really that transparent? That pathetic?

Giving a clipped nod, Andrew released his wrist and stepped back into the room.

He closed the door and leaned against it.

When had he become such a needy wreck? It hadn't been this bad even on the island—at least he didn't think it had been. Granted, in the past few months on the island, he had spent practically every minute with Logan, so there hadn't really been an opportunity to miss him and be clingy. The one time he'd woken up and found Logan gone—he remembered Logan holding him tightly and rubbing his back as Andrew clung to him like an octopus—it had freaked him out at the time, but it hadn't happened again, with Logan always warning him before he went away.

Andrew ran a hand over his warm face, shaking his head in bewilderment. Maybe he really needed a therapist. Maybe he should ask Logan to take him to a therapist—

Fucking hell. He really needed help.

Sighing, Andrew shrugged off Logan's jacket and headed to the ensuite.

A hot shower made him feel a little more like a human being. He was just finishing getting dressed when the door opened and Logan entered the room.

They stared at each other, Andrew's hands going still on the button of his shirt.

Logan was the one to break the silence. "You don't have to worry about my employees. They won't talk."

"I'm not worried," Andrew said.

The look Logan shot him was skeptical, but he didn't argue.

They stared at each other some more.

It was strange.

They'd spent an entire day in bed, not an inch between them, having sex pretty much nonstop like animals in mating season, and yet as soon as the haze of want was gone, there was this wary tension between them that refused to go away.

They were two very different men who knew each other inside and out. They were somehow too intimate and too apart at the same time. It was a paradox. And it drove Andrew crazy.

This need inside him, this need for Logan's closeness, was the scariest thing he'd ever felt, but at the same time it felt like the most natural thing in the world to need him. It really fucking messed with his head.

"I need to see a therapist," Andrew said.

Logan's dark brows furrowed. "Now?"

"Yes," Andrew said firmly. He hesitated. "Will you go with me?"

He hoped he sounded neutral instead of pleading, but judging by the softening of Logan's expression, he had failed.

Logan nodded and reached for his jacket.

***

Dr. Gillian Black was a middle-aged woman with a pleasant, friendly demeanor.

She invited Andrew and Logan to sit down on the comfy couch in her equally comfy office. She listened without interrupting as Andrew stumbled his way through the explanation of their problem.

Logan was silent at his side, his knee almost brushing Andrew's. Almost. Andrew shouldn't have been so fixated on the inch that separated their knees. It shouldn't have distracted him so much, but it did, and he kept losing his train of thought, because the need to have Logan a little closer was *eating* at him.

Finally, Andrew finished talking, and silence fell over the room.

"Well, the issue is rather obvious," Dr. Gillian said at last, watching them with her sharp gray eyes. "You went through a very difficult experience together. You were isolated from the world for nearly a year. Codependency is to be expected in such circumstances."

Andrew gave her an inpatient look. They weren't there to listen to the obvious. He wanted a solution. He wanted to be cured.

Logan's knee pressed against his, and Andrew breathed out, some of the tension leaving him. All right, he would be patient.

"But it's almost worse now than it was on the island," Andrew said, without looking at Logan.

She nodded. "It's not surprising. You went from being each other's everything to being nothing. Of course it's traumatic—it's too sudden. I wouldn't recommend abrupt separation. Gradual lessening of contact and intimacy should work better."

"What do you mean?" Logan said, speaking for the first time.

His knee was still pressed against Andrew's, a comforting pressure that settled something inside him.

Dr. Gillian looked at Logan. "Try to make your interactions not just about the two of you. Spend time together but with other people there too. Go for long walks in public places. Visit your friends and family together. Try to reclaim your normal routine. Gradually, the need for each other should lessen as you get used to other people until finally it will be completely gone."

Andrew frowned and looked away. "We've already gone to see my aunt together. It didn't exactly help."

"It's not enough, Andrew," she said. "You have to be patient. There's no magical cure for your situation. It might take months before you'll learn to stop needing each other. But it'll happen sooner the more effort you both make to reintegrate yourselves back into society."

Andrew pursed his lips. Months? Was she serious?

He looked at Logan. His expression was as grim and unhappy as Andrew felt.

"Thank you, Doctor," Logan said, getting to his feet.

They left the therapist, feeling even more lost than when they'd arrived. At least Andrew did. He wasn't sure what Logan was thinking, and it unsettled him.

He couldn't help shooting the other man sideways looks as Logan started the car.

Logan's profile was like a stone, impossible to read.

"Where are we going?" Andrew said.

"The airport."

His stomach tied up into knots. "The airport?"

Logan gave a clipped nod, his gaze on the road. "I'm returning to New York."

"But the therapist said…" Andrew cringed, hating how small his voice sounded.

"I know what the therapist said. I'm following her instructions."

Andrew chewed on his bottom lip, confused. "I don't understand."

Logan heaved a sigh. "She made it clear there's no quick solution to the issue. But I can't hang out here indefinitely. I can run my business from here too, but first I need to go back to New York to delegate some of my responsibilities and get my things."

"Get your things?" Andrew said, turning his head to him. He stared. "You're moving to Boston?" *For me?*

A muscle jumped in Logan's unshaven cheek. He wouldn't look at Andrew. "It isn't a big deal," he said stiffly. "My family is here, too."

Right. Of course.

Andrew's mind was still reeling. He folded his hands in his lap and stared at them.

When will you be back?

The question hovered on the tip of his tongue, but he bit it back. He didn't want to be that clingy. He was already acting pathetic as it was.

They arrived at the Boston airport way too soon.

"Here."

Andrew lifted his gaze.

Logan was giving him the car key. There was a strange look in his dark eyes as he gazed at Andrew. "Drive the car back to the hotel," he said, taking Andrew's hand and putting the key into his palm. "It's mine, not the hotel's. You can use it, if you need it."

His hand didn't move away immediately, causing goosebumps to run up Andrew's arm. His fingers started to tremble, clinging to Logan's of their own volition.

Logan looked down at them, his gaze so very dark, before looking back into Andrew's eyes.

"I'll be back soon," he said, his voice dropping to a hoarse whisper.

Andrew nodded numbly.

Logan untangled their fingers and opened the car door, letting the outside noise in.

Andrew grabbed his arm.

His muscles tensing, Logan turned back to him.

Andrew darted forward and buried his face against the hollow of Logan's throat. "I'm sorry for being such a mess," he whispered, inhaling his scent greedily.
He despised himself for acting like a junkie with a bad case of addiction whose drug was about to be taken away. But God, Logan smelled so good. Andrew wasn't even sure what he smelled like, but he smelled perfect. "I'm sorry," he repeated, gripping Logan's biceps. "I'm sorry I'm making your life harder and being—"

"Shut up," Logan said roughly, squeezing him with his arms. "We'll figure it out." He dropped a kiss on top of Andrew's head and took an audible breath. Then he pulled away and got out of the car.

Andrew stared at his wide back until Logan's tall figure was swallowed by the crowd.

Chapter 20

Andrew would like to say he did something productive with his time after Logan left, but that would be a lie.

He would like to say that he made an effort to be sociable, but that would be a lie, too. No, he pretty much lived in his hotel room and was the definition of a couch potato. He didn't talk to anyone, because he ignored his aunt's calls, and no one else ever called him.

It had never been more glaringly obvious that he didn't have friends. All of his friends had always been more of Vivian's than his. With her gone, clearly none of them gave enough of a damn about Andrew to even text him, much less call him.

You can call them yourself, Logan's sardonic voice said in his head.

Andrew groaned and flung an arm over his face. Even his inner voice sounded like Logan these days. He was hopeless.

His phone's ringtone made him flinch. Andrew sighed, thinking it was probably Aunt Rebecca again. He fished his phone out of his pocket and glanced at the Caller ID, just in case.

It was Shawn.

After a moment's hesitation, he answered.

"Hey," Shawn said, his voice a little tense.

"Hi."

"Um, how are you?"

Andrew's eyebrows went up. Really? "I'm fine, thanks," he said.

A pause.

"You've been kind of AWOL, buddy," Shawn said at last, answering his unasked question.

"I'm enjoying some peace and quiet," Andrew said. "Is there any reason you're calling me?" *You wouldn't call me if you didn't need something from me.*

"Uh, yeah," Shawn said, his tone hesitant.

Andrew smiled bitterly.

"Ian Caldwell's woken up from his coma," Shawn said.

Andrew stared at the ceiling, completely indifferent to the news.

"And? What do you want?"

"Derek would like your advice on how to proceed," Shawn said.

Andrew snorted, skeptical. "He does? Since when?"

"All right, no, but you know how proud he is." Shawn sounded fond and a little exasperated. "I know he feels guilty for landing the company in this mess, and he's determined to fix everything himself, even though it's out of his area of expertise."

That sounded more like Derek Rutledge.

A control freak.

An arrogant dick.

"I'm afraid he won't be able to crush Caldwell with the force of his personality," Andrew said, very dryly. "I had the pleasure of dealing with Caldwell a few years ago. He's as assertive as Derek."

"I know." Shawn sighed. "Which is why I need you to talk some sense into Derek. He's been talking to some lawyers. Please tell Derek he should try to make peace with the guy instead of going to war with him."

"Why me? He sure as hell cares about your opinion more than he cares about mine."

"Yes," Shawn said. "But he trusts your expertise in this matter. He trusts you to run the company well. He knows how capable you are."

Andrew opened his mouth and then closed it, not sure what to say.

"Then why isn't he the one calling me?" he said after a moment.

"I already told you why. He thinks it's his fault, and he's determined to..."

There was the sound of the lock being activated.

Andrew stared at the door handle as it turned, his heart starting to beat faster and his palms going clammy.

The door opened, and Logan stood in the doorway, looking at him with a strange, fixed expression on his face.

Shawn was still saying something, but Andrew couldn't hear it anymore, his pulse thundering in his ears and his world narrowing to Logan's dark eyes. There was something hard in them as Logan locked the door and walked toward him slowly.

Andrew wet his lips. It felt like every cell in his body was trying to jump out of his skin, and it took every bit of his strength to remain still on the bed.

Logan sat down beside him, still gazing at him strangely. Andrew couldn't fucking stand it anymore.He grabbed Logan's hand and jerked him closer. Logan fell on top of him awkwardly, crushing the breath out of his lungs, but Andrew didn't care.

He wrapped all his limbs around him, nearly moaning from how good it felt. *Finally*. He was here. Finally.

"Andrew?" said a muffled voice from his phone—the phone he'd dropped on the bed.

"I think you were in the middle of a conversation," Logan murmured, mouthing the side of his neck before sucking a hickey there.

Andrew shivered, whimpering. He buried his fingers in Logan's hair, pulling him closer. *Tighter. Need you closer.* "Huh?" he said breathlessly, pushing Logan's dark sweater off and running his hands greedily over the warm, smooth expanse of his back, kneading the firm muscle. "Missed you," he whispered before he could stop himself. "Need you."

Logan shuddered. He nipped his way up Andrew's neck and across his chin. He paused, their panting mouths hovering an inch apart. Andrew licked his trembling lips again, needing so badly he was literally shaking with it.

Fuck it.

He grabbed Logan's head and yanked him down into a hungry kiss.

God.

Although it was their first kiss, it felt like they'd done this hundreds of times already. It felt beyond perfect, his toes curling and his heart melting and his body trying to merge into Logan's. He'd never wanted anyone more.

They kissed and kissed, and it got rougher and needier, and then it wasn't enough.

Soon, their clothes were on the floor.

They fucked just like that, their lips locked together, Logan's hastily slicked-up cock moving in him with filthy, wet sounds of flesh against flesh.

Andrew wasn't even embarrassed of the high-pitched moans leaving his mouth as they fucked. He didn't care. He couldn't stop kissing him. Couldn't get enough of him. Couldn't touch him enough. He could die happily like this, full of Logan's cock and being kissed within an inch of his life.

He came too fast, sobbing and clinging to Logan's heavy body with all his might. It was bliss. It was pure heaven.

He didn't even mind that Logan kept fucking him for a while, no matter how oversensitive his hole now was. It still felt pleasant in a different way. It made him want to preen, Logan's every groan and moan like a personal accomplishment. He was wanted. He was needed. He was making Logan feel good.

When Logan finally spilled inside him and went still, Andrew was almost disappointed that it was over.

He had no idea how long they lay like that, floating on a post-orgasmic high.

It took Andrew a while to register something hard digging into his side. Frowning, he opened his eyes and retrieved the offending object.

His phone.

"Fuck."

Logan lifted his head and looked down at him, his eyes still a little glassy. "What?"

Andrew winced when he saw the length of the call. He was pretty sure he hadn't spoken to Shawn for seven minutes. How much had that asshole heard before hanging up?

"My brother-in-law's husband likely heard us having sex." Andrew sighed, running a hand over his face. "Fuck, did I say your name?"

When Logan didn't reply, he looked back at him.

Logan's expression was unreadable, but his brown eyes were significantly harder now. "And that would be a problem? Because I'm a man?"

Andrew pulled a face. "It's not… it's not really about that. I just really hate the idea of someone listening to me having sex. It makes me feel…" He winced again. "Kind of dirty. I've always been uncomfortable with public displays of affection, and this is far weirder. Sex is… I know it's old-fashioned, but I've always thought of sex as something private." Vivian had always made fun of him for being such a "prude," and although he'd disagreed, there was some truth to it.

He looked back at Logan, expecting him to make fun of him too, but the expression on his face wasn't mocking. Andrew wasn't sure *what* it was, but mockery wasn't there.

Logan laid a hand on Andrew's face, rubbing his cheek with his thumb for a moment. Andrew shivered, trying not to lean into the touch like a cat.

At last, Logan said, looking him in the eyes, "Even if he heard something, he wasn't here. He didn't see anything. It was just you and me."

Andrew swallowed.

"You and me," he repeated, and somehow, the words turned into something he hadn't intended them to be, and the air between them grew thick and heavy. Andrew found himself blushing, for no damn reason.

Logan's lips curled into a smile. It was a beautiful smile.

Andrew felt… He felt… Logan seemed too far all of a sudden; Andrew needed him closer. He buried his hand in Logan's hair and dragged him down into a hard, needy kiss.

God, he wanted to consume him, take his body into his own and keep it there, forever.

You and me, the words echoed in his mind as he sucked on Logan's tongue hungrily.

You and me, you and me, you and me.

Chapter 21

Andrew's mouth was fucking made for kissing, Logan thought. His lips were plump and soft, and he kissed with endless need that went straight to Logan's cock—and did uncomfortable things to his heart too.

Fuck, this was worse than the sex. Sex was just sex. Logan didn't have a problem separating sex from attachment and affection. But they weren't having sex now, and yet he was kissing Andrew. Just because he wanted it. Just because he loved feeling Andrew shiver in his arms, his trembling lips clinging to Logan's, Andrew's soft moans swallowed by his own mouth. There was something addictive about it. Something intoxicating. Logan felt drunk on these kisses, drunk and powerful, the pleasure unlike anything he'd ever felt.

They'd been kissing for what felt like hours, ever since they'd woken up. They'd already had morning sex, but they hadn't stopped kissing—the kisses just went from heated to lazy and clingy. Logan felt clingy as hell and it was starting to creep him out.

The sound of an incoming message broke the warm, intimate atmosphere in the room.

Andrew sighed and tore his mouth away with an obscene wet sound. Logan stared at those pink, moist lips as their owner reached for his phone.

Those pretty lips pursed slightly when Andrew saw the message. "It's Shawn again," he said. "He's inviting me for lunch."

Logan lifted his gaze. "You want to go?"

Andrew pulled a funny face, raking a hand through his messy curls. Fuck, he looked… Obviously he looked ridiculously sexy, all flushed and fucked out—but he also looked endearingly thoughtful.

Endearingly.

Christ, he was screwed.

"I don't know," Andrew said and caught his bottom lip between his teeth, looking down. He sighed. "I don't want to go, but I probably have to. I need to stop Vivian's brother from doing something potentially disastrous—again."

"Hm."

Andrew looked at him. "What?"

"You don't owe those people anything," Logan said, carefully keeping his tone neutral. "You don't have to do anything if you don't want to."

Andrew's brows furrowed. There was something almost like bewilderment in his eyes, as if he didn't even understand the concept.

"I need to do it," Andrew said, shaking his head. He set his jaw stubbornly. "Not because I think I owe something to the Rutledges. It's my company, too. I've worked my ass off for it for a decade. I'm not letting anyone ruin it, be it Caldwell or Derek."

Logan suppressed a smile. "Okay," he said. He glanced at his watch. "It's eleven already. You should probably be heading out soon."

Andrew frowned and dropped his gaze, his fingers anxiously playing with the sheets beneath him.

When he looked up again, his face was difficult to read. "Didn't the therapist say we should do stuff together?"

Logan stared at him. "You want me to go with you to your brother-in-law's house?"

A faint flush appeared on Andrew's cheekbones. "It's not that I want to. I just—I just want to follow the doctor's instructions and… Isn't that what we both want? Become normal again."

Normal.

Logan sat up, turning his back to Andrew, and said, "Fine."

Behind him, Andrew was quiet.

Logan stared at the condoms peeking out of his jeans' pocket. He'd forgotten to use them again. Irresponsible as hell. But then again, "irresponsible" was a good word to describe this clusterfuck of a relationship. God, what were they doing?

"Are you…" Andrew paused. "Are you mad at me?"

Logan's lips thinned.

"Why do you care even if I am?" he said tersely.

He felt the mattress dip as Andrew shifted, pressing his chest against Logan's bare back, his arms wrapping around Logan's middle. Logan sat very still.

Andrew sighed, burying his face in Logan's nape. He breathed in audibly. "I don't want to care," he whispered. "But you know I do." He gave a brittle laugh. "I care too much; that's the problem. Until we become normal again, I—" His voice cracked. "I can't fucking stand the thought of you being mad at me and leaving. I need you. Help me to stop needing you. And I'll get out of your hair, I promise."

Logan stared at the opposite wall. "All right."

Andrew kissed the back of his neck and let out a contented little sigh that did terrible things to Logan's heart.

Goddammit.

***

"I'll say we're friends," Andrew said as they approached the front door.

Logan snorted without looking at him. "I remember. You don't have to keep repeating it."

"I just—"

"Don't worry, no one will suspect that you rode my dick all night," Logan said, very dryly.

Flushing, Andrew hushed him, and just in time: the Rutledges' butler opened the door.

Logan followed Andrew into the large house, keeping a step behind him as Andrew greeted the handsome blond—Shawn—and his husband, Derek.

He watched the exchange curiously. Andrew was trying to look confident and calm, but his discomfort was obvious, at least to Logan.

The Rutledge couple was a little more difficult to read. The older man's face was stern and vaguely displeased, but his displeasure seemed directed at his own husband rather than at Andrew or Logan. It didn't take a genius to guess that inviting Andrew had been Shawn's idea and Derek didn't entirely approve of it.

It didn't seem to escape Andrew's notice, either: his body language became stiffer.

Logan stepped closer, their shoulders briefly knocking together as he stretched his hand out for a handshake. "Logan McCall."

The Rutledges shook his hand, eyeing him with some curiosity.

"Nice to meet you," Shawn said with a smile. "Andrew didn't tell me he was bringing a guest." His expression was open and friendly. Not a hint of suspicion in his eyes, only amicability. It seemed Andrew's fears were unfounded and Shawn hadn't actually overheard anything. Logan smiled back but didn't say anything.

Andrew shrugged. "My therapist recommended that we spend some time together to make the adjustment to our normal lives easier."

Shawn's brows knitted together but he just nodded, elbowing his husband discreetly when the latter remained silent.

"You're welcome to stay for lunch, of course," Derek said, glancing at his watch. "But I have my lawyer coming over, too." He shot Shawn a flat look. "I hope you won't be bored too much."

His husband just smiled innocently.

Logan suppressed a laugh. The couple was rather unconventional, but they seemed to suit each other. The affection, the warmth between them was real.

Watching them made him feel a little wistful.

He glanced at Andrew and quickly looked away, irritated with himself. Sometimes he hated his own brain.

"I'd actually like to be present at the meeting if it's about the company," Andrew said.

His tone sounded confident—*sounded* being the key word. Logan wasn't sure what it said about him that he could pick up the smallest shift in Andrew's voice, and could tell without even looking that Andrew wasn't actually as confident as he was trying to sound.

Derek gave a clipped nod just as the doorbell rang.

The lawyer was a handsome, well-dressed man with sharp gray eyes. He exchanged polite greetings with the Rutledges before turning to Andrew. "Andrew!" he said, his familiar tone making it obvious that he and Andrew were already well acquainted. "It's so good to see you—good to know that all those rumors were wrong."

"What rumors, Colt?" Andrew said, smiling neutrally. He had his arms crossed over his chest.

The lawyer made a face and clapped him on the shoulder, completely failing to notice Andrew's clear discomfort—or choosing to ignore it. "You've barely been seen since your return, practically turned into a hermit, and the usual people are talking. You know how it is."

Andrew's lips curled. "I know."

Colt's eyes shifted to Logan and lit up. He smiled and shook Logan's hand. "Oh, there's no need to introduce yourself—of course I recognize you, Mr. McCall."

"Logan is fine," he said curtly.

The guy's smile widened. "Then you should call me Colin," he said, his voice dropping slightly. "Colt is the nickname Vivian gave me."

Logan eyed him impassively. Colin was clearly interested in men, if the subtle once-over he gave Logan was any indication. The guy wasn't unattractive. He was possibly even more handsome than Andrew was. And yet, Logan didn't feel even a flicker of interest. Nothing. Not lust, not desire, not even mild appreciation. It was... concerning.

"You were friends with Andrew's wife?" he said politely.

"I was," Colin said, sighing. His gaze remained on Logan, however. "Such a tragedy. She was so young."

Andrew cleared his throat, touching Logan's arm. "Colin is—was Vivian's childhood friend," he said, gripping Logan's bicep a little too hard.

"Indeed," Colin said, his gaze flicking to Andrew's hand on Logan's arm. "I see you two became friends on that dreadful island… I have to say I'm surprised."

"Why?" Andrew said tersely.

Colin shrugged. "I thought you would be sick of each other by now." He smiled amicably at Andrew. "No offense, buddy, but we all know you can be a little… exhausting."

Andrew's face went utterly blank.

Logan had to suppress the ridiculous urge to pull Andrew close. Friends. They were here as friends, nothing more. Because they *weren't* more, dammit. Andrew didn't need him to act like a protective boyfriend.

"He's no more exhausting than you and me," Logan still found himself saying, though he kept his voice neutral.

Frowning, Colin looked sharply at Logan, then at Andrew, whose face no longer looked like a wooden mask. Andrew glanced at Logan and then quickly averted his gaze.

The tips of his ears were red.

Shawn coughed slightly. "The food is ready. Shall we?"

***

Logan had thought he would be bored. He had thought he would be forced to make some small talk with Shawn while Derek, Colin, and Andrew talked business. And in some way, he really was bored: most of the stuff they were discussing flew right over his head, because they were referencing people he didn't know and legal terms that barely made sense out of context.

But neither Andrew nor Colin seemed willing to leave him out of the strange pissing contest they had going, their biting remarks becoming progressively less subtle and progressively unprofessional the longer the meal lasted.

Even Derek was frowning now, his dark eyes flicking from Andrew to Colin in a sharp, assessing manner.

Logan was sipping his coffee and trying to pretend Andrew wasn't half in his lap. The more heated the discussion became, the closer to him Andrew seemed to gravitate. Their chairs had been a good few inches apart at the beginning of the meal, but now they were so close their thighs were pressed together. When Andrew got particularly nervous or angry, he hooked their ankles together, almost painfully so—all the while not looking at Logan at all.

Talk about mixed messages.

"…No, going public with this would be a bad move," Andrew was saying, glaring at Colin. "Are you an idiot? Caldwell did nothing wrong, technically, and even if we argue that Derek signed the contract under false pretenses, Derek did publicly dump Caldwell's sister, causing her to attempt *suicide*, so reminding of it will be bad publicity for us. Not to mention that Caldwell is a man who just woke up from a coma. You don't start a media war with a sick man! That's a bad look."

Colin didn't even bother hiding his condescending sneer. "We don't have to make it public. We can talk to him and pressure him into withdrawing. I'm sure he cares about his business reputation. He wouldn't want to be known as someone who makes underhanded deals."

Andrew laughed.

"So you're suggesting we threaten him? That's your professional advice? And you call yourself a lawyer? Ian Caldwell isn't exactly a man you threaten."

Colin flushed and opened his mouth, but whatever he was going to say was cut off by a cold, "Enough."

Everyone's gaze turned to their host.

Derek Rutledge's expression was rather sour as he pinned Andrew with a hard look. "What are you suggesting, then?"

Andrew's hand gripped Logan's knee under the table, but outwardly, his face was calm and confident. "I'm suggesting you talk to him."

"Talk to him," Derek repeated flatly.

Andrew let out a laugh. "I know: a wild concept, isn't it? Talk to him and apologize. Have you even tried?"

Derek's jaw clenched. "I have nothing to apologize for. If my actions caused harm, it wasn't intentional. The engagement wasn't my idea."

"Then *tell* him that," Andrew said. "Explain to him what really happened. What do you have to lose? Caldwell has something of a temper, but he isn't unreasonable. All of this seems like a case of a misunderstanding."

"I agree," Shawn said. "Maybe it's worth a try, Derek. If Miles is in love with the guy, surely he can't be that bad."

Derek's expression was rather pinched, but he didn't outright refuse. "I'll think about it," he said tersely, getting to his feet. Everyone followed suit.

Andrew's goodbyes to the Rutledges were rather stiff. He said nothing to Colin and strode out of the house without waiting for Logan to finish thanking the Rutledges for their hospitality.

But the moment Logan shut the front door behind him, he was yanked to the side, shoved against the wall, and suddenly had Andrew trying to tuck himself under his chin, breathing oddly. Hyperventilating.

It took Logan a moment to recover from his surprise.

Then, he wrapped his arms around him, and Andrew made a small sound—something pained but relieved too. Lips pressed against the hollow of Logan's throat. "Sorry," Andrew murmured into his neck. "It was just—it was hard for me to be around them, especially Colin. I know they all wish Vivian were here instead of me."

Logan frowned. "I'm sure they don't."

Andrew let out a humorless laugh. "Right. Did you see the way Colin looked at me? I'm sure he blames me for not saving her."

"Colin… What's the story there?" Logan said, threading his fingers through Andrew's curls.

Andrew sighed, stroking Logan's chest absentmindedly. "He was basically Vivian's childhood sweetheart. They were apparently on something of a break when I first met him. He made a move on me at a corporate party—he's bi—and I might have been… a little rude when I said I wasn't interested in men."

Logan could imagine it all too well. "And then what?"

"Well, he didn't take it well." Andrew pulled back a little, running a hand over his eyes. "A month later, Vivian and I started seeing each other, and imagine my surprise when she introduced me to her best friend-slash-ex. It was a little awkward, to say the least. For multiple reasons."

Logan knew he probably shouldn't have laughed, but it *was* funny, especially the face Andrew was pulling.

"Ha-fucking-ha," Andrew deadpanned, but the corners of his mouth twitched, and then he was laughing, too.

And Logan stared.

He had never seen Andrew laugh. Not like this: with pure mirth on his face, his eyes bright and soft, and his smile blinding.

He was beautiful.

It was the first time he thought of Andrew as beautiful. Handsome, hot, attractive, lovely—yes, but never beautiful. Beauty came from within; it wasn't just a physical attribute.

But fuck, he was beautiful, all laughing eyes, wild curls, and cherry red lips.

And Logan loved him.

He loved him.

"What?" Andrew said, smiling. "Why are you looking at me that way?"

Later. He could freak out later.

"No reason," Logan said hoarsely, pulling Andrew closer and kissing him.

Andrew's lips parted for his tongue immediately, and the world around them faded away—until the slam of the door made them flinch and break the kiss.

Logan turned his head and found himself looking at Colin's sneering face.

"Not a homo, huh?" Colin said, glaring at Andrew. "You didn't waste time after Vivian's death."

Andrew jumped away from Logan as though he'd been burned. "I—It isn't what it looks like!"

Logan suddenly felt cold, and it had little to do with the chilly November weather.

Colin scoffed and stalked toward his car. He slammed its door hard and took off, leaving a deafening silence in his wake.

It isn't what it looks like.

Logan bit the inside of his cheek so hard he tasted blood.

It shouldn't have hurt.

It shouldn't have mattered.

It wasn't like he hadn't known that Andrew would never want people to find out about them. He'd *known*. He'd always known he shouldn't allow himself to get attached to a "straight" guy. He'd known it would only lead to heartbreak if he was stupid enough to fall for Andrew. He'd known.

Idiot. He was an idiot.

"All right, I can't do it," he said without looking at Andrew.

"Do what?"

Logan suddenly craved a cigarette. It'd been years since he'd quit, but he'd never wanted to smoke this badly.

He shoved his hands into the pockets of his jacket. "Us," he said.

"I… I don't understand." Andrew's voice was so small that Logan had to stop himself from looking at him. Looking at him would be a terrible fucking idea. He was weak. He could never say no whenever Andrew looked at him in that particular way, his eyes wide and lips trembling.

"I've been out for nearly twenty years, Drew," he said quietly, looking at his car. "I'm not going back into the closet for you—for anyone. I'm not going to be your dirty little secret and live a lie while you act like we're nothing to each other in public. I'm too damn old for this shit."

There was only silence in response, heavy and tense.

Sighing, Logan headed to his car.

He didn't get far: Andrew's hand grabbed his arm. "But the therapist said—"

"I know," Logan said, his back to him. Andrew's touch seemed to be burning him even through the layers of fabric.

He wanted to turn around and take him into his arms.

He wanted to look into Andrew's eyes and allow himself to feel things he had no business feeling, not for this man. "And I'm sorry. I know it's hard for you. It's hard for me, too. I thought I could do this, but I was wrong. We'll only be making a bigger mistake if we continue living in each other's pockets." He ran a hand over his face, his voice dropping. "I can't do it, okay? I'm not a goddamn robot, Drew."

"But..." Andrew whispered, his voice barely audible. "But I need you."

Logan's chest hurt. "I need you, too," he admitted. "But needing isn't enough. Need and want are different things, and you don't want this." *You don't want me.*

"And you do?" Andrew said, his grip on Logan's arm still unrelenting, almost painful.

I shouldn't.

Logan's throat felt raw. He knew it was goodbye, and part of him, the part that still considered this man an extension of himself, actively rebelled against the idea, refusing to accept it.

But he knew it was the right decision. The only correct decision. Andrew wasn't going to suddenly accept that he was interested in men—that the island had been more than just an unhealthy phase. He would always consider his feelings for Logan as something that needed to be cured. He would never agree to be in a gay relationship openly, and that would effectively force Logan back into the closet.

Then there would be mutual resentment and anger, which would eventually turn their already less-than-conventional relationship into a toxic one.

There was only one ending to their relationship, and it wasn't a happy one.

This, whatever it was between them, wasn't sustainable. It was better to end it now while his heart wasn't completely wrecked. It was better to end it before it was too late.

It might already be too late, a voice said at the back of his mind.

Logan ignored it. It was his heart talking. He didn't trust it, not anymore.

A clean break. They needed a clean break. And for that, he needed to push Andrew away. He needed to do something to stop Andrew from continuing to reach out to him. Something that would be impossible to mend. A definitive end.

"I don't, either," Logan said roughly. "I'm too old to get hung up on straight, closeted guys again. Been there, done that. Too much of a mess to bother with."

Andrew's grip on his arm slackened. And then it was gone.

Logan headed to his car, his heart heavy and his stomach in hard knots.

He got into the car and started the engine. He drove away, barely seeing in front of him.

He told himself he'd done the right thing.

He *knew* he'd done the right thing.

It did nothing to alleviate the hollow feeling in his chest.

Turn back, a voice at the back of his mind said insistently.

Grab him and shackle him to you if you need to. Brand your name on him. He's yours. Yours yours yours.

Setting his jaw, Logan shoved those thoughts away. Andrew had never been his. He couldn't lose something he'd never really had. He couldn't deny that part of him had expected—hoped—that Andrew would finally say that he wanted him and ask him to stay. But Andrew hadn't.

If you love something, let it go. If it comes back, it's yours. If it doesn't, it never was.

Logan's lips curled into a humorless smile. Such a trite expression. Until now, he'd never understood it.

Chapter 22

Sometimes Shawn really hated having to act as a mediator. Be the patient one. The reasonable one.

Softening Derek's hard edges hadn't become any easier in the six years they'd been together. Though, he wasn't being entirely fair: Derek *had* mellowed out, somewhat. He wasn't the insufferable, bossy asshole he had once been—most of the time. The problem was, there were still times Derek relapsed to his old ways and the arrogant dick Shawn had fallen in love with all those years ago was back, to Shawn's fond aggravation. God, he loved this man, but there were still times Derek's behavior made him roll his eyes, sigh, and just shake his head.

Case in point: Andrew, and Derek's unwillingness to ask for his help.

"Pride is a sin, you know," Shawn murmured, his head on Derek's shoulder. He might have been annoyed with his husband right now, but he still wanted to cuddle up to him.

To his credit, Derek didn't pretend not to understand him. "Is it? Being a sinner doesn't bother me." His eyes remained on his tablet, his hand stroking Shawn's arm absentmindedly. It had no right to feel so good.

"You need his help," Shawn pressed, trying to focus on the conversation instead of the pleasant feeling spreading through his body from Derek's touch. "Now that Caldwell is back from England, it's time to finally bury the hatchet. For Miles's sake. You know the poor guy feels caught between us."

Derek's lips curled a little. "Maybe the kid shouldn't have slept with the enemy, then."

Shawn chuckled. "You know I don't like Caldwell, either, but now I think Andrew might be right. Maybe talking honestly and apologizing would actually work." Noticing Derek's grimace, Shawn chuckled again and pecked him on the stubbled cheek. "I know, I know: you have an allergy to apologizing and communicating your honest thoughts, but don't be a child, Derek."

The unimpressed look Derek shot him made him smile. "Look," Shawn said. "I know that… I know the subject isn't an easy one for you, with your father and all, but this is a situation that really can be fixed with a simple conversation. I talked to Miles today. He says he can make Caldwell listen to what you have to say. It will be—"

"Fine," Derek said testily. "Even if I talk to Caldwell, what do I need Andrew for?"

"Because he's an impartial party. He was there when you broke the engagement, and with your father and sister gone, he's the only person alive who knows why it happened, and everyone knows Andrew isn't exactly your fan so he won't lie about it. Caldwell will believe him."

Derek rubbed his forehead with his knuckles, looking like he was actually considering it, thank fuck.

"You're forgetting something," he said at last. "Andrew isn't in any state to be useful. He's little better than a walking corpse."

Shawn grimaced. That was a little bit harsh, but unfortunately, not really inaccurate.

He had never exactly liked Andrew after the less-than-stellar first impression he'd gotten all those years ago, but seeing him moving around listlessly with a vacant expression was highly unsettling.

The puzzling part was, Andrew seemed to have been getting better—he definitely seemed more put together at the lunch with Derek's lawyer a few months ago. Now he was much worse. Disinterested. Dejected. Miserable. Unwilling to talk to people. The only reason Shawn saw him at all was because he'd insisted that Andrew move back into their house when they found out he had still been living at a hotel. It had surprised him at the time that Andrew hadn't put up much of a fight, but by now Shawn knew better: the guy simply wasn't present enough to care.

"He's depressed," Shawn said. "Vivian's death—"

Derek scoffed. "Don't be naive. It's not about Vivian—at least not only."

Shawn looked at him curiously. "What do you mean?"

"McCall."

Frowning, Shawn said, "Logan McCall? What about him?"

"Andrew tried to make it seem as though they were friends, but their body language wasn't that of friends."

Shawn's mouth fell open. "What? You mean Andrew and Logan—"

"Probably fucked, yes." Derek gave a short laugh. "Two healthy men isolated on an island for nearly a year, frustrated and stressed. Are you really surprised?"

Shawn shook his head, his mind reeling. He suddenly remembered the strange noises he'd overheard when he'd called Andrew months ago. They'd almost sounded like… kissing. He'd been confused at the time, but he'd thought that it was the TV in Andrew's room.

"But Andrew is—"

"Straight?" Derek said dryly. "I recall you being straight, too."

"Homophobic," Shawn finished, giving him an unimpressed look.

Derek hummed thoughtfully. "He's always been so outspoken about it… You know, it's always made me wonder if he was overcompensating. Either way, he and McCall had the body language of lovers. I'm pretty sure he was holding McCall's hand under the table."

Shawn looked at him skeptically. He couldn't imagine Andrew—the bigoted asshole Andrew—holding a man's hand. "Are you saying he's moping because of Logan?"

Derek shrugged. "He seemed fine when McCall was around. The next time we saw him, McCall was nowhere to be seen and he looked like a depressed mess."

"You're reaching," Shawn said, still skeptical.

Derek smiled at him, his dark eyes full of amusement. "Your gaydar is just shit, Wyatt."

"Rutledge," Shawn corrected with a grin before kissing him. Soon enough, all thoughts about Andrew completely left his mind.

There was only Derek.

***

Rebecca Kennett was annoyed. Annoyed, displeased, and worried.

There was something wrong with her nephew.

His apathy wasn't normal. She had thought his depression was caused by his wife's death and it would pass soon enough, but Andrew wasn't getting better. No, he'd been getting worse. He seemed to have completely lost his drive, his ambition—and sometimes she had the disturbing thought that he had lost his will to live.

It scared her.

Rebecca wasn't an affectionate woman—she didn't really know how to show affection—but it didn't mean she didn't care for the boy. She may not have given birth to him, but she had raised him since he was a scrawny three-year-old. She had given up her personal life for him, her ambitions and dreams. The ungrateful boy had no right to make her worry so much.

After Andrew failed to turn up at her house on Christmas and then missed her birthday—something he had never done before—Rebecca had had enough.

She overcame her distaste and went looking for him at the Rutledges' mansion. She had little doubt that Andrew had chosen this place because he knew how much she disliked those people. Well, the stupid boy had underestimated the lengths she was willing to go to for him. She even managed a polite conversation with Shawn Rutledge before he finally led her to Andrew's room.

"I really hope you can help him," he said. "He's freaking me out. He hasn't left his room for days."

Rebecca pursed her lips and gave a tight nod.

She entered the room.

The first thing that hit her was the smell—a pungent combination of alcohol, dried vomit, and body odor.

Grimacing in distaste, Rebecca walked to the bed and glared at the man in it. "I have never been more disappointed in my life."

Andrew focused his glassy eyes on her. "Auntie!" he slurred. "Sorry for not getting up for you. Did you want something from me?"

"You're pathetic," Rebecca said bitingly. "What is the meaning of this? Why are you drunk in the middle of the day?"

Andrew took a sip from his bottle of vodka. "Why not? Not like anyone cares."

I do, she nearly snapped at him.

She didn't say it. Trying to reason with drunk men was useless.

Rebecca stepped closer and tugged the bottle out of his hand. "You will stop drinking at once. You will take a shower and shave. You will then go downstairs and eat. After that, I'm taking you to a therapist."

Andrew laughed harshly. "Not going to any therapists. Charlatans, they are." He laughed again. "I'm talking like Yoda now, huh."

"You're not amusing. Get up."

Andrew didn't move. He stared at her with sudden seriousness in his gaze, his smile gone. He seemed sober all of a sudden. "Why do you care?" he said. "You don't, not really."

Rebecca glared at him. "Don't tell me what I do or don't feel, boy. Get up. Now."

A smile curled Andrew's lips. There was something bitter about it. Something sour. "If I told you the truth, you'd stop caring very fast, Auntie."

"I'm losing my patience, Andrew—"

"I had another man's dick up my ass. I sucked a dick and loved it."

She stared at him.

He stared back at her, something defiant, hard, and broken in his gaze.

Rebecca said, "Get up and take a shower."

He blinked, confusion written all over his face.

She would have laughed if there were anything amusing about the situation.

Did he think her an idiot?

Did he think she hadn't noticed the way he had looked at that man?

"What?" he said in a small voice, sounding very much like the little boy he'd once been.

She looked away for a moment. "Your sexual experiments, however ill-advised they may be, don't interest me. Now get up."

He stared at her. "What if… What if I told you that it isn't just an experiment?"

She pursed her lips tightly. She didn't want to have this conversation. She had hoped they would never need to have this conversation. "If you're trying to say that you're obsessed with that man, don't waste your time. I'm not blind. But it will pass. It's a product of your enforced closeness on that island; that's all. It's understandable that you're confused. You just miss your wife, Andrew."

He looked away and stared at the ceiling blankly. "Confused. Right."

"It's of no relevance. Pull yourself together. Your wife was an amazing woman, but she's gone. You're not. Now stop being so pathetic and get up." She half-regretted her harsh words as soon as she said them, but she'd never been good at showing affection, no matter how much she cared. Giving comfort had never been Rebecca's strong point—too much stored bitterness of her own to carry around; never mind anyone else's pain.

He got up.

Watching him sway on his feet made her heart clench. How had they come to this? He'd always been such a good, smart boy. She'd always taught him to be as self-sufficient as she was. Had she failed? Where had she gone wrong? He shouldn't have been such a mess after losing his wife.

Millions of men lost their spouses and went on with their lives. Was this the survivor's guilt?

Unless... unless this was about more than just Vivian. Could he need someone to love him to feel his own worth?

The thought was highly unsettling, but it refused to disappear, no matter how much she pushed it away.

"Andrew," she said when he finally reached the door.

He paused, his hand on the door handle.

"I do care for you," she said stiffly. "I love you. I wouldn't be here if I didn't. You do know that, right?"

He turned his head and looked at her over his shoulder.

His blue-green eyes were glistening as he nodded.

Chapter 23

It was the middle of February when Andrew woke up to the sound of birds chirping outside the window.

He listened to it for a while before realizing that something had changed. Gone was the numbness, the feeling of wrongness on the inside that he'd been carrying for months.

He lay in the bed he'd shared with Vivian for nearly a decade, listening to himself. The mattress wasn't too soft. The sheets didn't feel too smooth. The sun filtering through the curtains illuminated the room in a soft glow, and it wasn't an annoyance. Andrew felt... okay.

He was okay.

He wasn't sure why. Maybe talking to the therapist his aunt had forced on him really was helping, or maybe his aunt trying to show him affection in her own stilted, awkward way was the reason he felt better. Or maybe it was true that time healed everything. Or maybe it was a combination of those things. Either way, he felt different, in a good way.

Andrew sat up slowly, still half-dreading that the familiar depression and disconnect would come back.

But nothing happened.

He was still okay.

A slow, uncertain smile curled his lips.

Andrew got out of the bed and opened the curtains, and then opened the window, allowing the sun to touch his face. It was warm.

He laughed, just because he could.

He felt warm, for the first time in months.

***

The first thing he did was go to his barber and have his wild curls trimmed. It was a little strange to see himself look like his old self after such a long time, but it wasn't a bad feeling.

He was finally moving on. He was leaving the island behind. It was… It was a good thing.

Andrew left the barber with a spring in his step.

The people on the busy sidewalk kept bumping into him, but he didn't mind. He no longer felt like an alien among them. He finally felt like he was one of them, maybe. There was still some discomfort from being around so many people, but it was nothing too bad. He felt like he could get used to it.

He really was okay.

***

His positive attitude lasted.

Even the meeting between Caldwell and Derek that took place a few days later didn't manage to ruin it. Andrew found himself feeling surprisingly patient as he mediated between them.

But fuck, why were all rich, powerful men such asses? Listening to Derek stiffly explaining himself was aggravating. Encouraging him to clarify and clarifying things for him whenever Derek refused to was beyond aggravating. It was like pulling teeth. Caldwell's cold, dismissive attitude was just as aggravating.

Andrew was pretty proud of himself for managing not to snap at either of them.

When the excruciating meeting was finally over and Caldwell and Derek had agreed to a tentative truce, Andrew felt like it was his personal accomplishment. It surely wasn't thanks to Derek. Andrew was the one who had ended up doing most of the explaining and apologizing, until the ice in Caldwell's eyes finally thawed. It really felt like a personal win.

Never mind that he didn't actually win anything: Caldwell would remain the CEO of both companies, so strictly speaking, Andrew wasn't getting his job back. That said, he would be the COO and run Rutledge Enterprises on a day-to-day basis, so effectively, he got the job back— just without all the perks of officially being the boss.

Although Caldwell would still be the CEO, he'd be taking a step back from business for his family for a while. Apparently he wanted to spend more time with his son— the poor kid needed it after having his dad in a coma for months. Andrew and Raffaele Ferrara were going to have to take on Caldwell's responsibilities in Rutledge Enterprises and the Caldwell Group respectively, with Caldwell attending only the most important meetings.

Surprisingly, Andrew didn't mind the solution.

Or maybe it wasn't all that surprising. He'd never wanted power for the sake of it. He'd hated that he had been overlooked by the old Rutledge in favor of his estranged son, had hated feeling like a toy discarded in favor of a new one—and that had been pretty much it. He had enjoyed being the CEO, enjoyed feeling necessary and having his employees look up at him with admiration. He would still have that. And at the end of the day, Derek and Caldwell had *chosen* him to run the company.

They trusted him. It was enough.

So Andrew was in a pretty damn good mood as he left Caldwell's office. Derek had left a while ago while Andrew had stayed to discuss practicalities with Caldwell, but they were finally done. He could go home and—

He collided with another guy outside the office, hard.

"Bloody hell—sorry, I wasn't looking where I was going," said the guy. He was young and handsome, and he had a distinct British accent.

"It's fine," Andrew said, still feeling in a good enough mood to be charitable. He was also pleased that he didn't feel uncomfortable with an unfamiliar person in his personal space.

The guy smiled and held out his hand. "I'm Miles. You work for Ian?"

Andrew shook it. "Andrew Reyes." It took him a moment to register the question. Right. He did work for Ian Caldwell now, though it was a little surprising that such a young guy was referring to the CEO with such familiarity. "I've worked for this company for a decade," he said, studying the guy for a moment and not recognizing him at all. "You must be new?"

Miles shook his head with a laugh. "Oh, I don't work here—not anymore, at least." He paused, and then said, blushing a little, "I'm Ian's boyfriend."

Andrew stared.

Part of him, the part that could think rationally, vaguely recalled hearing Shawn and Derek mentioning someone named Miles, but he hadn't been interested enough to care at the time.

"Oh," he said. "I thought…"

Miles smiled crookedly. "You thought Ian was straight," he stated, pulling a funny face.

"We get that a lot." His gaze became sharper. "Is that a problem?"

"No," Andrew said after a moment. "I'm just surprised, that's all."

Miles nodded, his expression softening again. "Okay, see you around, then," he said with a smile before striding into the office. He pushed the door closed, but it didn't shut all the way.

Andrew didn't intend to eavesdrop. He was simply standing there, feeling frozen, as he listened to the couple inside the office. There was some laughter, Caldwell's cold voice sounding noticeably warmer, and then there was the sound of kissing. A soft moan.

"Mmm, I missed you," Miles said, followed by more kissing sounds.

Andrew bit his bottom lip hard, staring at the opposite wall unseeingly.

"It's been just a few hours," Caldwell said with a laugh before his voice became serious. "How was it?"

"It was… okay. A little awkward, but better than I expected. Your sister even smiled at me by the end of the lunch. Well, almost smiled, but I take it as a win. Baby steps. Rome wasn't built in a day."

Caldwell sighed. "You must regret leaving the UK for this shit."

"I didn't leave the UK for this shit." Miles's voice was soft. "I left it for you, but it doesn't make me some kind of self-sacrificing martyr. It was actually a pretty selfish decision. I want to be with you because you make me happy. Very selfish, isn't it?"

Caldwell chuckled, and then there were more sounds of kissing.

Andrew slowly moved away.

His chest felt tight. Achy.

I want to be with you because you make me happy.

Such simple words, but they hurt.

The ache in his chest aside, it wasn't pleasant to realize that he'd been lying to himself. He felt foolish now. Delusional. He had been so determined to get his old life back that he had somehow failed to realize that it may not have been possible at all, that he may not have been the same person at all.

He might not have been a depressed mess anymore, but he wasn't the Andrew Reyes he had been a year ago. He couldn't be that person again. The island had changed him. His old beliefs and emotions felt so distant now. He didn't think the same way. He didn't feel the same way. If a year ago he'd overheard Ian Caldwell kissing some guy in his office, Andrew would have sneered. He would have felt disgusted, not… whatever the tight feeling in his chest was.

Coward, a voice said at the back of his mind. *You know what you're feeling. Envy. Jealousy. Yearning.*

Heartache.

Andrew closed the door of the restroom behind him and staggered to the sink. He opened the tap and splashed cold water on his face.

"I just miss Vivian," he whispered.

Coward, the voice said again. *It's not her you miss.*

"Shut up." He felt like a madman, talking to himself. Maybe he *was* mad. Maybe all of this wasn't real and he would wake up any moment, curled up in Logan's arms—

The *yearning* that hit him was so strong that Andrew had to bite his lip, his eyes tearing up.

God, he hated himself. He'd thought he was finally past this. He'd thought he was finally cured of him. But it seemed all he'd managed to accomplish was to push Logan to the back of his mind and suppress, suppress, suppress. Being okay wasn't the same as being happy.

I want to be with you because you make me happy.

The door behind him opened. "Andrew?"

Andrew lifted his gaze and met a pair of concerned blue eyes in the mirror. Right. Nate. Raffaele Ferrara's assistant.

He blinked the wetness away from his eyes, hoping it wasn't obvious that he'd been this close to crying. "Hey. Were you looking for me?" he said, pretty proud that his voice sounded normal enough. "Did Caldwell already tell you that I'd be running the company? You're probably going to be my assistant."

Nate snorted softly, walking to a urinal. "I know about the decision Caldwell made, but I'm not going to be your PA. I wish, but my dick of a boss would never let his favorite whipping boy walk free. I'm not the CEO's assistant. I'm his. He's taking me with him back to the Caldwell Group."

Andrew averted his gaze when Nate unzipped his pants. "How did you know about the decision, then? The meeting ended just ten minutes ago."

Nate made an amused sound. "The meeting with Rutledge didn't actually decide anything. Caldwell's boyfriend had already talked him into leaving the Rutledges alone."

Miles?

Andrew frowned. "What? But… How do you even know so much about it?" It wasn't exactly public knowledge that Caldwell had wanted revenge on the Rutledges.

Nate zipped up. "Caldwell is friends with my boss. I heard them discuss it yesterday."

Yesterday?

Andrew scowled. Why had Caldwell even forced Derek and him to go through the excruciating ordeal of apologizing for Derek's actions if he'd already made the decision?

As if reading his thoughts, Nate chuckled. "Caldwell might have already made the decision, but it doesn't mean he didn't still want to make Rutledge grovel. He's an asshole, though not as big of an asshole as my asshole of a boss. Mine is Satan personified."

Andrew shot him a curious glance. "Why don't you quit if Ferrara is that bad?"

Nate's face did something strange. He shrugged and went to the sink to wash his hands. "So, why were you crying?"

The sudden change of subject caught Andrew off guard. "I wasn't," he said after a moment, painfully aware of how unconvincing it must have sounded.

Nate gave him a long look. "You can talk to me, you know. I've been told I'm a pretty good listener."

Andrew's first urge was to say that he was fine and change the subject.

But then he hesitated.

Why not, really? Nate wasn't even going to work in their company anymore. He wasn't going to be Andrew's subordinate. And he seemed like a good guy, his face open and his blue eyes kind. Andrew couldn't deny that he wanted a fresh perspective, wanted to talk to someone—*anyone*. He felt like he'd explode if he didn't talk about this to someone. His therapist didn't count, and all of his friends had been Vivian's.

"Have you ever been with a man?" He flushed as soon as he blurted it out.

Nate blinked, his golden eyebrows slightly raised. "I'm straight," he said. "The closest I've been to another guy's cock was when my demon of a boss made me put a condom on his."

Andrew stared at him. And then stared some more. "Eh, what?"

Nate laughed. It wasn't a very amused sound. "I know, right? My boss is a fucking psycho. I swear he lives to torture me. Not only do I have to buy condoms for him—among a million other tasks—but he also literally made me put a condom on his cock before he fucked some leggy blonde with a fake tan and fake boobs." He scowled. "He's—" He cut himself off and shook his head. Then he looked at Andrew curiously. "So, what's with the sudden interest? What does it have to do with your crying?"

"I wasn't crying," Andrew said.

Nate's silence said it all.

Running a hand over his face, Andrew sighed. He looked around the room before returning his gaze to Nate. "You know I was stuck on the island with another man, right?"

Nate's forehead wrinkled. "Everyone knows that—Wait. Are you saying you and Logan McCall...?"

Andrew face felt very warm. He was already starting to regret speaking of this, but he couldn't backtrack now. "Yeah," he said, uncomfortably. "It was just a stress thing."

Nate nodded, his expression understanding. "You were lonely."

"Yeah." Andrew looked down at his hands. They were pale again, he noted dispassionately. His tan was long gone. "Lonely, desperate, and scared. And he was the only thing that kept me semi-sane. He was—he was my everything back then. But it was supposed to go away once we…"

"Ah."

They were silent for a while.

Andrew couldn't look at the other guy as he confessed roughly, "I was supposed to—was supposed to stop needing him. My life is good now. I'm okay. I shouldn't still need him."

"Why not?" Nate said quietly. "Because it's gay?"

"It's not… It's not really that. I used to think that way, but not anymore. I *can't* feel that way for real, not about him."

"Why not?" Nate sounded puzzled. "What's wrong with needing the person you're in love with?"

Andrew opened his mouth. No sound came out of it.

"I'm not in love with him," he managed at last. Of course he wasn't in love with Logan. What a ridiculous idea. Right?

"I don't know," Nate said, radiating skepticism. "You seem pretty heartbroken."

"I'm heartbroken because I'm grieving my wife."

"You have no reason to feel guilty, you know," Nate said, not unkindly. "She's been gone for over a year."

Andrew turned away from Nate and stared at his own reflection. Pale. He was so pale, his eyes the only color on his face.

"You know why I feel guilty?" he said hoarsely. "Why what I feel for him can't be normal? I loved Vivian, I adored her, but if someone told me that I could have either Vivian or him back…" He swallowed. "I'm not at all sure I'd choose my wife. I wouldn't choose her."

There.

He'd finally said those words out loud.

The thought had been eating away at him for months, but he'd been holding it inside, still trying to pretend it wasn't real.

"Oh."

Andrew nearly laughed. Yes, *oh.* "So of course I fucking feel guilty. I'm the worst. She was my wife. My best friend. I loved her."

This couldn't be love. Dependency, need, obsession. Anything but love. He had loved Vivian. What he felt for Logan was so much more intense and raw. It couldn't possibly be something as normal as love, right? God, he wasn't sure of anything anymore.

It had been so comforting to think that it all had been just a phase, an unhealthy coping mechanism that would go away once he acclimated to the real world again. Well, he had acclimated to the real world, but nothing had changed about his feelings for Logan.

No, to be fair, something had changed. He was now able to function adequately without Logan. The problem was, he didn't *want* to. He no longer needed Logan for the world to make sense. He just needed him, period.

I want to be with you because you make me happy.

"Did you and Logan have a falling out?" Nate said, snapping him out of his thoughts.

Andrew sighed. "No—yes. Vivian's close friend saw us kissing, and I pushed Logan away and acted like it meant nothing. It pissed Logan off. He said he didn't like being forced back into the closet. He clearly thought I was just being a repressed, bigoted ass."

"And he was wrong?"

Andrew shrugged. "It wasn't… It wasn't really about that. I mean, my wife's funeral had been just the other week, and then her best friend sees me making out with someone else. It looked beyond shitty. So I overreacted when Colin saw us."

"Why didn't you explain that to Logan?"

Andrew laughed a little. "There was no point. He said he didn't want to deal with my mess anymore." He swallowed the lump in his throat. Tried to. "He said he didn't want me."

"And you believed him? If you weren't honest with him, what makes you think he was being honest with you?"

"It doesn't matter," Andrew said after a moment. "I'm not—I don't want to be a burden to someone who doesn't want me."

Nate made a thoughtful sound.

"I get it, but have you considered that it might have been just a misunderstanding? He misunderstood why you didn't want to be seen with him, got angry, and said that he didn't want you, either, just to protect himself. It's human nature."

Andrew frowned.

"Think about it," Nate said and left.

Chapter 24

Andrew thought about it.

It was all he thought about for the next two weeks.

Could Nate be right? Could Logan maybe not have meant it when he'd said he didn't want him?

He hated himself for even entertaining the thought, hated that he was unable to quash the hope that rose up in him.

He found himself staring at Logan's number at night, his thumb hovering over it until it was shaking with discomfort.

It was stupid. Even if Logan really had wanted him back then, he might have moved on by now. It had been nearly four months. And Andrew still had no idea if he could be honest with Logan about how he really felt when he could barely be honest with himself. *I can live without you, but I don't want to. I feel guilty that I need you more than I've ever needed my wife. I feel guilty, because I'm scared I wouldn't be happy even if I had her back.*

That night, he dreamed.

He dreamed of Vivian.

They were seated on the island's beach, her head on his shoulder.

Their fingers were intertwined.

It was peaceful. Quiet.

"I know you loved me," she said. "You made me the happiest woman in the world." She turned her head and looked at him with her lovely eyes. She smiled, touching his face. "It's okay. I want you to be happy, silly." She brushed her lips against his, the touch affectionate and warm. "Loving someone is always scary. But I know you're brave. Be brave, sweetheart."

And then she was gone.

Andrew woke up with tears in his eyes.

He lay like that, crying silently until there were no tears left.

He felt at peace, for the first time in a long time.

After a while, he reached for his phone and scrolled to his aunt's number. He hit Call.

"Andrew?" she said, sounding sleepy. "Is something wrong?"

Right. It was still early morning.

"It wasn't an experiment," he said hoarsely. "I think I'm bi."

There was silence on the line.

He could hear his aunt breathe unsteadily. "Andrew… Is this about that man?" she said. "Logan?"

Andrew stared at the ceiling. "It isn't about anyone. It's about me. I'm attracted to men. I want to know if you — if you can still — "

"Don't be stupid," she said tersely. "You think I dedicated my life to raising you just to — you think that's enough for me to give up on you?"

"It isn't?" he croaked out.

"Idiot boy," she bit off and hung up.

Andrew stared at the phone blankly before a laugh left his throat.

Something in his chest loosened a bit. He knew his aunt would never entirely approve of his sexuality, but maybe it was okay.

Maybe she didn't need to approve of his life choices to love him.

***

He had intended to be an adult about it.

He had wanted to message Logan with something neutral, find out where he was, if he was seeing anyone (even thinking about it made him feel *sick*, but it was a possibility, one he couldn't dismiss), but in the end, he was too much of a coward. He wasn't brave at all.

So Andrew did the responsible, adult thing: he stalked Logan.

He went back to Logan's hotel and asked the manager for his address. The manager recognized him this time, and after having seen Andrew nearly naked in Logan's room, probably had drawn his own conclusions and didn't need much convincing when Andrew said he wanted to surprise Logan. He got the address.

To his surprise, it was a Boston address. Apparently Logan hadn't returned to New York. Logan had been here all this time. So close. And yet he'd stayed away.

Andrew wasn't sure what to think. How to feel. Hell, he still wasn't sure what he was going to *say* when he saw Logan again.

As he approached the house, he played out various scenarios in his head.

Realistically, he knew that Logan was unlikely to be happy to see him. He knew it was a stupid idea to go there without any warning.

It was probably going to be awkward as fuck. It was likely that they had become strangers to each other. At best, there would be some awkward small talk. At worst, Logan would be angry with him for seeking him out. Or…

Enough, he told himself as he stopped in front of the door. *Whatever happens, happens. At least I'll get some closure and stop this stupid pining.*

He knocked.

It felt like forever before the door finally opened. Logan's slight smile froze when he saw Andrew.

All the words died in Andrew's throat.

He looked so good.

It was probably a stupid thought, because Logan always looked good, but Andrew didn't really mean his looks. The way he looked—his stubbled face, his dark eyes, the sardonic curl of his firm mouth—it was… Logan looked like home. He looked like *his,* Andrew's.

Later, Andrew would be embarrassed by what he did.

Later, he would be mortified. Right now he didn't give a damn—he just wanted.

He practically launched himself at Logan and kissed him hard, his hands running up and down Logan's arms, over his broad shoulders and strong back, wanting to feel him, needing him so much he was shaking with it. He kissed him desperately, all teeth and tongue, craving him, breathing in his scent like an addict, and unable to get enough.

At first Logan didn't respond, his body rigid with tension. But then, he groaned and kissed back, his arm crushing Andrew against his chest and his other hand burying in Andrew's hair. God, it felt so good, so perfect, so right.

Andrew's eyes were burning with tears, his lips—his everything—clinging to Logan, unable to let go, unwilling to let go, *never again.*

There was some noise, but Andrew barely registered it, his body boneless against Logan, his mouth insatiable, every part of his being singing with happiness. God, the way he smelled, the way he tasted, it was—

"Ahem," someone said again. "Do we need to go, brother? We can go."

Andrew whined when Logan stopped kissing him, seeking his mouth blindly. *No, don't go.*

"Christ," Logan said and kissed him again, pulling their hips flush.

"Eh, maybe get a room, you two," a laughing female voice said.

When the words fully registered, Andrew tried to wrench his lips away from Logan's, but this time it was Logan who didn't let him, kissing him again, and again, and again, his mouth wet, hot, and hungry, his hands kneading Andrew's ass.

"I hate to interrupt, I really do, but this is getting really awkward, brother mine." The voice sounded really close now, and Andrew tore his mouth away with a miserable whimper and forced his eyes open.

Even when his eyes finally managed to focus on the smiling woman behind Logan, it took him a few moments to recognize her. Right. Logan's sister. *Both* of his sisters. Both of his sisters and half a dozen unfamiliar people that looked a lot like Logan. People who all were staring at Andrew and had undoubtedly just witnessed Andrew jumping Logan and groping him all over. Great. It was a good thing he was already flushed and it wasn't physically possible for Andrew to blush harder.

He said faintly, "Hey."

"Hi, Andrew," the woman said. Was it Kate or Alice? They kind of looked alike, and Andrew's hazy brain still wasn't exactly at its best. To be honest, it took everything in him not to go back to clinging to Logan. Other people's scrutiny wasn't exactly helping his equilibrium. He still couldn't bring himself to step away from Logan.

Logan stood very still beside him.

Andrew risked a glance at him and found himself caught in those dark eyes again.

They were difficult to read, but they remained only on Andrew. "What are you doing here?" he said quietly, ignoring his relatives completely.

Andrew moistened his lips with his tongue, and felt a surge of happiness when Logan's gaze flicked down to his mouth before he visibly forced himself to return it back to Andrew's eyes.

Logan still wanted him. Except physical want meant very little.

The thought made Andrew deflate. He looked at Logan's face searchingly, but it was difficult to read him.

"Are you going to introduce us, son?" said a female voice.

Logan glanced at the people in his house before looking back at Andrew. "This is Andrew Reyes," he said, his voice stiff, uncharacteristically hesitant for him.

"We are aware of his name," said the same woman. Logan's mother. She seemed to be in her sixties, her gaze not unkind but bewildered as she eyed Andrew.

The unsaid question was clear. *Who is he to you?*

Andrew swallowed. He looked at Logan uncertainly, but Logan's expression was unreadable.

Guarded.

He was still gazing at Andrew intently, but he wasn't in a hurry to reply to the unasked question.

Andrew's heart seemed to be beating somewhere in his throat. He swallowed again. Part of him wanted to remain silent—until Logan indicated that he actually wanted them to be something. But he had a feeling that it would be a mistake.

Needing isn't enough, Logan had told him months ago. *You don't want this.*

He was pretty sure Logan wanted him to take the first step.

But if he was wrong, if Logan didn't actually want to be with him, this would be the worst humiliation of his life, humiliation his heart would never recover from.

He would have to make a leap of faith. Be brave for once. Do something the bigoted man he had been a year ago would have never done.

Andrew took a deep breath. Then he looked at Logan's mother, because it was easier, and said, "I'm Logan's boyfriend."

The surprised silence that fell over the room was deafening, but Andrew barely paid it any mind. All his senses were attuned to the man who stood very still beside him.

Finally, Andrew found the courage to look at him.

Logan's guarded expression had melted away. His dark eyes were warm, so very warm now, gazing at Andrew with a look that made Andrew's breath catch in his throat. Then a smile appeared, first in Logan's eyes before spreading to the rest of his face.

Logan pulled him close and gave him a hard, possessive kiss, his strong hands cradling Andrew's face gently.

"Boyfriend, huh?" he said, breaking the kiss and leaning their foreheads together. "Thanks for letting me know."

Blushing, Andrew laughed, wrapping his arms around Logan's neck and melting into him.

He didn't care that Logan's entire family was looking at them. He was happy. He felt whole, safe, and wanted.

He was where he wanted to be.

Epilogue

Three months later

Derek Rutledge stood on the terrace of his house, nursing a glass of wine and watching the guests milling about the garden. The formal part of the evening was over, and the journalists were gone. Thank fuck.

He loosened his tie with one hand, his eyes searching for his husband. Shawn was nowhere to be seen, which was fucking priceless, since the whole thing had been his idea.

A party in celebration of the one-year anniversary of the partnership will show everyone that there's no bad blood between us and Ian Caldwell, Shawn had said, looking at him with his annoyingly pretty eyes. The little shit knew exactly the effect they had on him: that they got Derek to agree to the most inane ideas.

To be fair, Shawn's idea had some merit. Despite their best efforts to keep their conflict quiet, people still talked. One of the lawyers Derek had consulted must have spilled the beans to the press, which had resulted in a lot of media scrutiny. Not to mention that it had somewhat hurt the business, since people were wary of dealing with a company that had unstable leadership at the top.

So here he was, pretending to be best friends with Ian Caldwell and his people. Not that they were enemies, per se.

Caldwell's attitude had thawed quite a bit ever since Derek had spoken to Caldwell's sister and told her the truth. It had been the most awkward conversation of his life, but Derek had to admit it had been long overdue. It'd helped. He and the Caldwells were quite civil these days, but some things weren't easy to forget, and Derek doubted they were going to become best friends anytime soon.

His lips twisting at the thought, he eyed the crowd in search of Shawn.

Caldwell was still there, his arm around Miles. The sight of them used to make Derek uneasy. He hadn't been sure Caldwell wasn't just using the kid to get to him, but by now even he had to admit that Caldwell seemed genuinely gone on Miles—which was clearly mutual. Miles was grinning at Caldwell right now, his hand touching the older man's chest in a rather proprietary manner. Neither of them seemed to care that they were in public, their eyes only on each other. Derek had to give it to Caldwell: for a formerly straight man, he didn't seem to mind being out and proud with Miles, uncaring what anyone else thought of him.

Though, Caldwell's openly homosexual relationship wasn't as surprising as Andrew's.

Derek shifted his gaze to his former brother-in-law and eyed him in slight bewilderment. Truth be told, he could barely recognize him as the man who had been his sister's husband. Vivian's husband had always acted like he had a giant stick up his ass. He had always looked at Shawn and him with a barely hidden sneer on his lips, his homophobia obvious. He had been a good husband to Vivian, which had been the only reason Derek had tolerated the man.

So now, seeing Andrew all but snuggled up to another man in public was surreal.

All right, "snuggled up" might have been something of an exaggeration, but still. Andrew was gazing at Logan McCall in a decidedly besotted manner as McCall said something to him before kissing the corner of Andrew's mouth. Andrew grabbed McCall's tie and pulled him closer, changing the kiss from innocent to needy, and never mind that there were plenty of people around. It seemed as though he'd forgotten that they weren't alone—or didn't care.

Shaking his head, Derek looked away from the couple and continued looking for Shawn among the guests. His gaze passed over Raffaele Ferrara, who stood by the pool nursing a drink. Ferrara had a beautiful woman on his arm, but he didn't seem to be paying her any attention, his black eyes fixed on something else, his body language faintly irritated.

There were footsteps behind him, and then arms wrapped around his waist.

Derek didn't turn.

"It's rude to hide from your own guests, Mr. Rutledge," Shawn said with a smile in his voice, pressing his cheek against Derek's shoulder from behind.

Derek took a sip of his wine. "You know I don't like parties."

Shawn chuckled, kissing the back of his neck. "Don't be such a grumpy old man. You're hardly old."

Putting his glass on the table nearby, Derek laid his arm over Shawn's and said, looking at the guests, "It's just strange." *To do what my father used to do, after avoiding this life for two decades.*

He didn't say it aloud, but of course Shawn understood. He always did. A little too well.

Humming, Shawn entwined their fingers together. "I definitely didn't expect to host fancy parties for billionaires when I went to my knees for a grade," he said, laughter in his voice. "Life can be weird that way."

Derek turned around and studied him. "Any regrets?"

Blue eyes smiled at him softly. "None," Shawn said, wrapping his arms around Derek's neck and fitting their mouths together. "Never."

***

Andrew was a clingy drunk. He was also a very horny one.

Logan laughed, catching Andrew's hand as it sneaked down to his dick. "Let's wait until we get home, Drew."

Andrew pouted, his blue-green eyes still fixed on Logan's face and entirely ignoring the party around them. "But I want you. Want your cock in me."

Christ.

Trying to ignore the way his boxers were suddenly too tight, Logan wrapped an arm around Andrew's waist and half-dragged him away from the party. "Let's get home, hm? And then you can tell me how much you want me."

"But I want you now," Andrew whined, pressing wet, open-mouthed kisses to Logan's jawline.

"I thought you hated PDA? People are staring. I don't want you to be embarrassed tomorrow when you sober up."

"Don't care," Andrew mumbled, nuzzling into Logan's neck. "Love you."

Logan's steps faltered. They'd… They'd never really talked about feelings. Andrew was his boyfriend, they lived together, and they were happier than Logan had thought was possible. Their relationship was going great, so he had decided not to rock the boat by confessing that he loved Andrew—Andrew's reactions could be so unpredictable sometimes. Logan hadn't expected to hear a confession from Andrew first.

"You're drunk," he said, clearing his throat.

"But I love you," Andrew murmured, sucking a hickey on Logan's neck. "So much. I feel like I'm choking on it sometimes. Got drunk to tell you. Am not brave enough sober."

Feeling a rush of overwhelming affection, Logan tipped Andrew's face up with his fingers.

"You don't need to get drunk for that, sweetheart," he said hoarsely, looking into Andrew's glassy eyes. "I love you, too."

Andrew's eyes widened, a flush appearing on his cheeks.

"Tell me that again in the morning?" he asked, in a small voice. "In case I forget."

Logan smiled at him gently. "I will," he said. "I will tell you that every day if you want."

Andrew beamed at him, his eyes glistening. "You promise?"

God, he was beyond endearing.

"I promise," Logan said, kissing him on the forehead.

Andrew hugged him. "Love you," he whispered, his lips brushing Logan's neck. "I'll always need you. Always."

"I know." Logan kissed the top of his head and smiled. "Me, too, love."

"I still hope I'll die before you," Andrew mumbled, and Logan suddenly remembered the conversation they'd had all those months ago, after Andrew's illness.

His throat uncomfortably thick, he buried his face in Andrew's hair. He breathed in. "Nope," he said hoarsely, his arms tightening. "You aren't allowed to die before me."

Andrew giggled. "I guess we'll have to die at the same time, then," he said, lifting his head and smiling at him.

Smiling back, Logan leaned their foreheads together. "I guess we'll have to."

It was probably strange how certain he was that they'd still be together decades from now.

It was stranger that a year and a half ago he hadn't known this man at all. Now he was his world.

"I've been thinking..." Logan said, rubbing his nose against Andrew's. Christ, sometimes he couldn't believe how sappy they were. He'd never been like this with any of his past boyfriends. It was a little embarrassing, truth be told. "What do you think about a vacation? Maybe on some tropical island—"

Andrew was still laughing when Logan kissed him.

The End

About the Author

Alessandra Hazard is the author of the bestselling MM romance series *Straight Guys*, *The Wrong Alpha*, and *Calluvia's Royalty*.

Visit Alessandra's website to learn more about her books: http://www.alessandrahazard.com/books/

To be notified when Alessandra's new books become available, you can subscribe to her mailing list: http://www.alessandrahazard.com/subscribe/

You can contact the author at her website or email her at author@alessandrahazard.com.